"I just wouldn't like us to become—close, and then discover a relationship between us is impossible."

Nathan pulled her into his arms. "We're already close, Brianna," he murmured huskily, his breath stirring the hair at her temple. "Didn't this morning prove that?"

CAROLE MORTIMER says: "I was born in England, the youngest of three children—I have two older brothers. I started writing in 1978, and have now written over ninety books for Harlequin Presents®.

"I have four sons—Matthew, Joshua, Timothy and Peter—and a bearded collie dog called Merlyn. I'm in a very happy relationship with Peter senior; we're best friends as well as lovers, which is probably the best recipe for a successful relationship. We live on the Isle of Man."

Books by Carole Mortimer

HARLEQUIN PRESENTS
1863—ONE-MAN WOMAN
1894—WILDEST DREAMS
1929—A MARRIAGE TO REMEMBER
1965—THE DIAMOND BRIDE

Carole Mortimer

Joined by Marriage

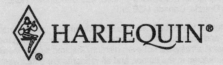

HARLEQUIN®

TORONTO • NEW YORK • LONDON
AMSTERDAM • PARIS • SYDNEY • HAMBURG
STOCKHOLM • ATHENS • TOKYO • MILAN • MADRID
PRAGUE • WARSAW • BUDAPEST • AUCKLAND

Peter,

Eternity

ISBN 0-373-11977-1

JOINED BY MARRIAGE

First North American Publication 1998.

Copyright © 1998 by Carole Mortimer.

Printed in U.S.A.

PROLOGUE

A SINGLE sheet of paper lay on the table in front of her, the words written upon it, as she looked down at them, at once seeming not enough and yet at the same time too much. Perhaps she shouldn't have written this letter. But a part of her had wanted to so much. She couldn't let go without leaving something, something to say that she had been here at all.

She picked up the letter and read it once more, unaware that her tears fell onto the paper. She had read the words so many times already, knew them all by heart. And yet she read them again, reluctant to let them go, too, now that the time had come.

Would they ever be read by the person she'd written them for, anyway?

Or would someone, perhaps someone wiser than her, deem it better that her letter be destroyed?

Slender fingers tightened on the sheet of paper as she held it to her protectively. It wouldn't be destroyed. It would reach the person it was intended for. It had to. It was all she had left to give. Of herself.

She had long since given up the emotional struggle as to whether what she was doing was right. She had taken that inevitable step some time ago. What was right and what was wrong had passed long since. And leaving this letter, whether right or wrong, was something she needed to do. Had to do.

Then do it, that warring voice inside her head instructed. Do it, and let that be an end to it.

An end...

This letter was the end.

Or a beginning...

CHAPTER ONE

THE letter was decidedly unhelpful, Brianna decided. It told her nothing. And yet at the same time it promised her everything.

> Dear Miss Gibson,
>   Could you please contact our office at the above address, either by telephone or mail, at your earliest convenience, so that we might arrange a time for you to call in and see one of our partners?

The notepaper heading was that of a firm of prestigious London lawyers, but the signature at the bottom of the short request wasn't that of any of the partners listed at the top of the letter.

Everything and nothing.

'What have you got there, sis?' Her brother Gary leant over her shoulder, the bowl of cereal he was eating for breakfast tipping precariously in the direction of Brianna's plate of toast as he did so.

Brianna reached up and straightened the bowl. 'A case of mistaken identity, I think,' she said dryly, crushing the letter into a ball in preparation for throwing it into the bin when she had finished eating.

'What's that, love?' her father said vaguely as he came into the kitchen straightening his tie, a tall, loose-limbed man in his early fifties.

She shook her head, smiling. 'Just a firm of lawyers who haven't done their homework very well and have sent a letter to me by mistake.' She stood up, the letter already forgotten. 'Would you like some toast for—Dad, what is it?' She frowned as she saw he hadn't moved to the refrigerator for his customary glass of early-morning orange juice but had come to a sudden halt just inside the kitchen door, his face pale. 'Dad?' she prompted again worriedly.

He sat down heavily on one of the chairs at the kitchen table. 'Could I see the letter?' he said abruptly.

'This?' Brianna looked down at the crumpled piece of paper in her hand. 'But I just told you, it's obviously a case of mistaken identity—'

'Landris, Landris and Davis,' her father said flatly, his gaze steadily meeting hers.

Her eyes widened as her father correctly named the firm of lawyers who had sent her the letter. How on earth—?

'Please, Brianna.' He held out his hand for the letter, then slowly and meticulously straightened out the creases before attempting to read its typed words.

'What's going on, sis?' Gary asked in a loud whisper, his cereal being eaten now as he got ready to leave for school. In his final year at school, and taking his 'A' levels, Gary looked like most of his peers: hair a bit too long, clothes studiously untidy, not yet a man but no longer a child.

'I have no idea,' Brianna told him frankly, distractedly handing him some money for his bus fare and lunch.

He grimaced at the way their father just sat looking at that letter Brianna had received in this morning's post. 'Looks serious,' he muttered.

Brianna wasn't altogether certain how it looked. And she wasn't sure she wanted to know, either. Her mother had died just over two years ago, and since that time their father, with help from Brianna, had managed to keep them going as a family.

Perhaps this letter was something to do with her mother? Although that didn't make much sense to her either; her mother had left them all that she had to give, which was her love, and the happiness of close-knit family life. That was a legacy not everyone could leave behind them.

'School,' she reminded her brother as he hovered curiously, then 'Homework,' as she handed him a folder from the top of the fridge. 'Bus,' she finished pointedly.

He looked disgruntled at having to miss finding out what the mystery was all about, and pulled a face as he went. But he was going to miss his bus if he didn't leave now, and having to walk the distance to school wouldn't suit him at all; any form of exercise was total anathema to Gary!

Brianna busied herself tidying away the breakfast dishes, knowing that when her father was ready he would talk to her. She had learnt this practice from her mother, although it hadn't been an easy lesson to learn; Brianna was more inclined to impulsive action than thinking things through. But, as her mother had pointed out affectionately long ago, her father could be led but he wouldn't be pushed.

And so Brianna waited—although she hoped her father wouldn't take too long over his musing, or the two of them were going to be late for work, her father at his consulting rooms, Brianna at the hospital where she worked as a receptionist.

Her father suddenly spoke, his voice gruff with emotion. 'I believe that this letter has something to do with your real mother.'

Brianna turned slowly, frowning. Her parents had never made any secret of the fact that she was adopted. It had been explained to her as soon as she was old enough to understand that she was special, a gift to

Graham and Jean Gibson after childless years of marriage.

It had never bothered Brianna that she was adopted or that, as often happened in these cases, her adoptive parents had actually conceived a baby of their own when she was four years old. She was 'special', loved all the more dearly because her parents had believed they would never have a child of their own. It was because of that love she had never felt any inclination to search out her real parents; she simply didn't feel the need to know them, accepting that there must have been a reason she was given away in the first place, and that it was probably a reason that might still cause hurt and distress to the people involved.

She had certainly never expected that her real mother would seek her out!

She sat down in the chair opposite her father, her face pale, blue eyes wide above a small nose, generous mouth, and stubbornly determined chin. Her father had often teased her about that stubbornness during her childhood, saying her shoulder-length hair should have been red rather than the colour of gold-ripened wheat. But gold it was, straight and fine to her shoulders, with a wispy fringe above those deep blue eyes.

'Why do you think that?' she asked through stiff lips. She didn't want to hear any of this!

Her father looked at her with steady brown eyes. 'Because I received a letter from them myself about three months ago. Just before your twenty-first birthday...'

'The letter clearly states that you should contact us before coming to the office,' the frosty middle-aged receptionist told her dismissively. 'I would be happy to make an appointment for you to see—'

'I don't want an appointment,' Brianna told her

equally coldly—after all, she was a receptionist herself, knew every put-off there was, both polite and otherwise. She also knew that if she waited here long enough, refusing to budge, someone would eventually see her. 'I wish to see one of the partners mentioned in the letter. Now.'

And she was determined that she would. She had been totally shocked this morning when her father had told her Landris, Landris and Davis had written to him some time ago, enquiring as to whether he had an adopted daughter by the name of Brianna. Her father had written back confirming that he did, and asked exactly why it was they wanted to know. But he had received no reply from the lawyers in the three months that followed and had finally decided the law firm must have made some sort of mistake. The second letter, this morning, from the same practice, seemed to indicate there had been no mistake after all...

Brianna had gone off to work as usual, but she had been distracted all morning, thoughts going round and round inside her head, and she'd finally decided that enough was enough. She hated mysteries, and the sooner she found an answer to this one, the better. Which was why she had taken a taxi to this office during her lunch-break.

The premises of Landris, Landris and Davis were designed to be imposing, the grey-haired dragon of a receptionist a further deterrent to anyone not here on serious business. Or someone without an appointment...

'I'm afraid that's impossible,' the woman told her firmly. 'None of the partners are available to see you at the moment.'

'Then I'll wait until one of them *is* available,' Brianna informed her stubbornly.

'Look, Miss—Gibson—' the woman filled in her

name after another quick glance at the letter Brianna had
received this morning '—I'm afraid it doesn't work that
way. I can make you an appointment, possibly some
time next week—'

'I don't think so,' Brianna cut in mildly, deep blue
eyes silently warring with stony brown.

'Miss Gibson, I really must insist—'

'Problems, Hazel?'

Both women turned sharply at the sound of that
deeply male voice, the receptionist at once looking flus-
tered and Brianna's interest in the intruder deepening as
she saw the other woman's reaction to him.

Not a simple clerk, by the look of him. He stood well
over six feet tall, and was powerfully built beneath the
formality of the dark suit and white shirt he wore. He
looked down his arrogant nose at the two of them with
icy blue eyes through dark-rimmed glasses: eyes that
were not the deep blue of Brianna's own, but a pale blue
that sent an arctic chill down her spine.

Some of the doctors she worked with on a day-to-day
basis were a little full of their own importance, but this
man's air of arrogance was nothing like theirs; it seemed
to be inborn and his air of severity was added to by the
shortness of his dark hair, his hard, chiselled features
and firm, unsmiling mouth. In fact, the man didn't look
as if he found much in life to smile about!

Brianna's irritation with the receptionist turned to pity
as she imagined having to work with the Ice Man day
in and day out...!

'No, not really, Mr Nathan,' the receptionist assured
him in a voice that seemed suddenly breathless, sound-
ing more like a little girl's than that of a mature woman
in her fifties. 'It's only that Miss Gibson doesn't have
an appointment—'

'Gibson?' He repeated the name in a clipped voice,

once again looking through those dark-rimmed glasses
down his thin, aristocratic nose at Brianna. 'Exactly who
is it you are wishing to see, Miss Gibson?'

Her father was right about her temper, and, as this
man not only looked down at her but spoke down to her
too, she could feel it rapidly rising. 'Landris, Landris or
Davis,' she returned, as coolly as he had spoken to her.

Irritation flickered across his aristocratic features, his
mouth twisting mockingly. 'That's rather a generalisa-
tion,' he drawled derisively.

Her eyes flashed. 'I can't be any more specific than
that. The letter I received from this office was just as
ambiguous,' she returned scathingly.

'Letter?' Those icy blue eyes narrowed behind the
glasses. 'What letter is that? Maybe if I could see it—'

'I have it here, Mr Nathan,' Hazel offered eagerly,
holding out what was turning out to be a much-read
letter.

'Mr Nathan' took it. His hands were long and slender—far too artistically sensitive for such a man,
Brianna decided critically.

She realised she had taken an instant dislike to him.
She usually got on with most people, that was why her
job at the hospital was so interesting and enjoyable.
Maybe it was just that she was already so emotionally
strung-out. After all, she didn't even know him, although
a part of her said she didn't want to, either!

'Hmm.' When he looked up again, his gaze was even
more chilly than before. 'It states quite clearly here
that—' He broke off as an elderly couple entered the
reception area. 'Would you like to come to my office,
Miss—Gibson?' This time *he* added her name after another glance at the letter, which he still held. 'We can
talk more privately there.'

The receptionist looked alarmed. 'You have an appointment at two o'clock, Mr Nathan.'

'Plenty of time, Hazel,' he dismissed with a wave of his hand, before taking a firm hold of Brianna's arm. 'If you would like to come this way, Miss Gibson,' he suggested as the elderly couple approached the receptionist desk. 'I'm sure you will be more comfortable in my office.'

And not such a visible nuisance, Brianna guessed wryly. It simply wasn't done, at the offices of Landris, Landris and Davis, to have altercations, no matter how mild, in their reception area.

She wasn't sure that 'comfortable' exactly described the room he took her into; grand and imposing sprang to mind, but not comfortable! The walls were panelled halfway up in the dark oak, and above hung paper the colour of a deep blue sky; there was a much darker blue carpet on the floor, and one of the walls was completely lined with books, all of them of legal origin, if the titles were anything to go by. In the centre of the room a huge bay window, edged with dark blue velvet curtains the same colour blue as the carpet formed the backdrop to a very wide oak desk. A high-backed dark blue leather chair sat behind it; a smaller chair in the same leather faced it.

Mr Nathan moved to sit in the large chair, indicating she should sit opposite him, her letter still firmly in his possession. He laid it down on the desk in front of him, reading it again quickly before looking up at her once again. 'You really have no idea what this letter is about?' he prompted.

She had only the guesswork of her father to go on, which she wasn't sure was accurate. She had been put up for adoption when she was only two months old, so why on earth should her real parents be interested in her now?

Although that first letter sent to her father by this firm of lawyers three months ago was still a puzzle...

'None,' she replied quickly.

He pursed his firm, unsmiling lips. 'I see,' he murmured thoughtfully.

'And I really think, Mr Nathan—' Brianna sat forward in her chair '—that if you don't know either, then you're wasting my time as well as your own!'

She felt the embarrassed colour enter her cheeks after this outburst, realising instantly that she owed him an apology; after all, he hadn't needed to bother with her at all, he could just have left her for the receptionist to deal with—which she was sure, without this man as an audience, the other woman was more than capable of doing!

'I'm sorry, Mr Nathan.' She sat back with a heavy sigh. 'It's just that letters like that one—' she indicated the letter in front of him '—arriving in the post without warning, can be quite unnerving.'

'I'm sure they can,' he returned smoothly. 'But could I just set the record straight on one thing before we continue this conversation?'

She looked across at him expectantly. 'Yes?'

He gave a small inclination of his head, the late spring sunlight coming through the window behind him showing a slight touch of red in the darkness. 'My name is not Mr Nathan.'

'But it's what the receptionist just called you,' Brianna protested confusedly.

His mouth quirked, not quite into a smile, but into something—in this man's case, Brianna felt—that came very close to it. 'It's what she has always called me.'

'But I don't see why, if it isn't your name.' Brianna frowned. 'You—'

'If you will just allow me to finish?' the man continued imperiously. 'Are you usually this—impetuous, Miss Gibson?' He frowned at her darkly, as if she were a species he very rarely came into contact with! And she didn't mean women; she was sure there was a wife in the background somewhere, someone as stiffly formal and haughty as he was. He obviously just wasn't used to someone as bluntly forthright as she was.

Well, that was okay, because she had never met anyone quite this stuffy and arrogant before, either. It wasn't even as if he was that old; possibly he was in his mid-thirties, and yet he talked and behaved like someone so much older than that. What he really needed was to—

Never mind what he needed, she impatiently admonished herself; she would never see him again after today, anyway. She wasn't going to get anything out of him at all if she didn't curb her impetuosity a little.

'Probably,' she conceded with a grimace. 'Otherwise I wouldn't have come here today at all, would I?' she added with a shrug.

His face showed his irritation with her levity. 'As I was saying...'

'Before you were so rudely interrupted!' Brianna couldn't control the facetious mental ending to his statement—or the smile that threatened to curve her lips and bring a sparkle to the deep blue of her eyes. The first she stifled by biting her bottom lip, the latter she could do nothing about, although she did make an effort to try and look avidly interested in what he was saying. If only he weren't so pompous...!

'Hazel calls me Mr Nathan because she has known me most of my life,' he bit out tersely, as if he guessed some of her amusement was at his expense.

'That sounds fair enough—except you've just told me it isn't your name!' Brianna shook her head frustratedly.

Maybe it was her, or maybe what he was saying had lost something in the translation—because for all she understood his explanation he might as well have been talking a foreign language! But if his name wasn't Mr Nathan, why on earth did the receptionist persist in calling him that?

He drew in a harshly controlling breath, studying her with narrowed eyes behind his dark-rimmed lenses, as if he sensed only too well that she was laughing at him.

Which she wasn't. Well, not really. She was sure she was the one missing something here; this man was far too sensible ever to talk the load of nonsense this conversation had so far seemed to her to be. No doubt he would explain properly in a minute, and all would be understood. She hoped...

'My name is Nathan.' He spoke slowly now, as if he were talking to a slightly backward child. 'And, as Hazel has worked on Reception here for the last thirty years, she has known me since I began visiting these offices when I was five years old.'

Brianna put her head back, looking puzzled. She still didn't understand, but she was beginning to think it wasn't her fault, after all...

'You've been a lawyer since you were five years old...?' she said in slow disbelief.

He scowled. 'You know, if I didn't think your bewilderment was genuine—'

'Oh, but I can assure you it is,' she hastily replied, not liking the dark clouds she could see appearing over his furrowed brow.

God, this man must be daunting in a court-room. But not since he was five years old... She didn't even know what had made her make such a ridiculous remark. A slight touch of hysteria probably. But not because of him; it was this situation over the letter that had her so wound up.

'Of course you haven't been a lawyer since you were five.' She dismissed her own stupidity. 'I'm just a little confused.'

He gave her a look that clearly said he thought she was *very* confused!

He absently moved the letter around the top of his desk before replying. 'I was visiting my father at these offices, Miss Gibson,' he bit out in those coldly clipped tones that were rapidly becoming familiar to her. 'He was—and still is—a lawyer.'

'Oh.' Brianna nodded, sure there was more to come. Although she was getting a little tired of waiting. They hadn't even really begun talking about her letter yet. Were all lawyers this pedantic?

'My first name is Nathan,' he finally explained. 'And since I came to work here Hazel has always called me Mr Nathan, simply as a sign of respect, I suppose. Although, in the circumstances, it's probably less confusing for her too,' he added thoughtfully, his icy blue gaze boring into Brianna as he looked at her steadily. 'My name is Nathan Landris, Miss Gibson,' he bit out.

At last! Nathan Landris. One of the partners... 'Which Landris are you—Landris or Landris?' She frowned.

'Neither,' he returned dryly. 'My father is Landris, and my uncle James was Landris—but he died ten years ago. And my uncle Roger is Davis.'

How extremely confusing. 'So you aren't Landris or Landris?'

'I'm afraid not,' he confirmed. 'In five years' time—'

'When you're forty?' Brianna quickly and instinctively calculated, still trying to come to terms with who this man was. Oh, she had decided very quickly that he

couldn't be anything as lowly as a clerk—this office he
had brought her into had only confirmed that—but she
certainly hadn't realised he was the son of one of the
partners in the firm. No wonder Hazel called him Mr
Nathan!

'When I'm forty,' he echoed curtly, again watching
her with narrowed eyes, as if uncertain whether or not
she was laughing at him.

Which she wasn't now. Okay, so he was pompous,
obviously took himself—and everything else—far too
seriously, but he was also the son of one of the partners
of this prestigious firm; getting as far as talking to him
had to be better than being turned away until 'possibly
some time next week' by the ever-vigilant Hazel.

'Then I'll be made into a full partner,' he informed
her crisply. 'And we will become Landris, Landris,
Davis—'

'And Landris,' Brianna finished knowingly.

What else? They couldn't possibly remain just
Landris, Landris, and Davis—oh, no, the fourth partner—despite the fact that one of their number was dead,
and his nephew's surname was the same—would have
to be officially added to the partnership.

It all sounded positively feudal to Brianna. But then,
other aspects of this law firm seemed slightly out of
time, anyway, this man opposite her along with them...
She could picture him now, as a feudal overlord, dis-
pensing law and wisdom with an arrogant flick of his
wrist or a raising of his eyebrow. He—

'Have you ever thought of taking up law yourself,
Miss Gibson?'

His speculative voice interrupted her wandering
thoughts and Brianna focused on him with effort, back
in the here and now, having been in the middle of imag-
ining him riding across his lands on a magnificent black

stallion, his hair neither as short nor as controlled as it was now, dressed in magnificent robes of blue and gold. Ridiculous. In reality, he was a stiff, unyielding man, full of his own importance.

And at this moment he was looking at her with cold impatience as he waited for her response to his remark!

'Sorry?' She blinked long dark lashes.

'The law, Miss Gibson,' he drawled derisively. 'I have a feeling you would make a formidable lawyer. I have never met you before today—in fact we have only been acquainted for ten minutes or so—and yet I seem to have talked to you of my childhood, my age, and my intention of being a partner here by the time I'm forty.' He shook his head in denial of such intimacy with a relative stranger. 'But, at the same time, I know little or nothing about you. Quite remarkable, Miss Gibson,' he added.

'Brianna,' she supplied absently, grinning as he raised his brows questioningly. 'As we seem to have become such confidantes,' she added teasingly, 'you may as well call me Brianna.'

'Your name is Brianna?' he said slowly.

Almost disbelievingly, it seemed to her. 'Of course it's my name,' she snapped. 'I would hardly have said so otherwise, now would I?' Not everyone suffered such confusion over their name as this man did!

'I didn't mean to sound offensive, Miss—Brianna—'

He didn't mean to—he just was!

'It's just that it's an unusual name.' He frowned darkly. 'Almost masculine.'

'Well, I can assure you—I'm not!' she bit out impatiently, wishing she had never told him her first name; he was making such a meal out of it!

His mouth once again twisted into what Brianna assured herself must be a smile—although it looked more like a pained grimace to her. 'I can see that.' He dryly acknowledged her prettily petite but definitely feminine figure in a fitted skirt and neat, fitted blue blouse tucked in at her slender waistband.

He showed as much male awareness of her as a woman as a stick might, Brianna decided. And time was pressing; she would be late back to work if she didn't soon settle this.

'Maybe I had a male relative named Brian; I really don't know,' she dismissed. 'No one has ever bothered to explain.' She glanced at her wristwatch; she really would have to leave soon. 'I'm afraid, Mr Landris, that if you can't help me—'

'I'm afraid I can't.' Without her being aware of it, he had stood up and was even now moving around his desk, as if to escort her to the door. 'It really would be better if you made an appointment with Hazel. It's my father you want to see.'

Brianna felt as if she was being swept along in the middle of a tidal wave as he clasped her arm, once she had stood to her feet, and began walking her toward the door. But she came to an abrupt halt at this last remark, looking up at him suspiciously. 'How do you know that?' He hadn't known it in the reception area. Or, at least, he hadn't appeared to…

He shrugged broad shoulders beneath the dark suit he wore. 'The reference at the top of the letter is obviously his.'

He had known exactly who the letter was from, and which Landris she should have seen! Her eyes flashed accusingly; she was getting more than a little tired of the feeling of being shunted from one person to another, with none of them more willing to be of help to her than the last. What was the mystery, for goodness' sake? *She* was the one who had been sent the letter; she hadn't come here uninvited!

Brianna snatched the letter out of his hand, glaring up at him. 'Why didn't you just tell me from the first that it's your father I need to see?'

'Because he isn't here at the moment,' Nathan Landris answered firmly. 'But I'm sure Hazel told you that...?'

'She said he wasn't available,' Brianna scorned, 'whatever that's supposed to mean!' She wasn't sure any more!

Icy blue eyes unwaveringly met deep blue. 'It means he isn't available,' Nathan clipped. 'But I'll tell him you called.'

'Will you?' she challenged; she had the feeling this man wanted to forget ever setting eyes on her! In this case the feeling was mutual. Pompous, overbearing, bossy—

'Yes, I'll tell him,' Nathan Landris confirmed dryly. 'But I suggest you make an appointment with Hazel, nonetheless.'

'For "some time next week",' she said disgustedly.

He gave a haughty inclination of his head. 'If that's the first appointment available to you, then, yes.'

Brianna looked at him. 'Despite what you said earlier about my own qualities, Mr Landris, I have a feeling you're quite formidable yourself in a court-room!' she said slowly.

He gave what could only be described as a wolf-like smile—that of one which had just pounced on its prey! 'I have been known to win the odd case or so,' he drawled.

She bet he had—he'd certainly managed to effectively divert her from her initial purpose here! 'I'm sure,' she accepted scathingly. 'If you'll excuse me.' She walked to the door. 'It seems I have an appointment to make!'

She turned and stormed out of the office, neither thanking him—she had no reason to do so!—or saying goodbye. Somehow she had a feeling, despite the fact that there was absolutely no reason why they should, that they would meet again...

'I'll come with you.'

Brianna turned to him in the carpeted corridor. 'There's no need for you to do that—I'm not about to steal the company silver!'

He looked down at her from his imposing height, dark brows raised reprovingly. 'Are you always this—forthright, Miss Gibson?' he said carefully.

'Probably,' she dismissed. 'I suppose, despite what you said earlier, that excludes me from taking up law as a profession?'

The insult hung in the air between them, only a nerve pulsing high in Nathan Landris's cheek, as he reached up to remove his glasses, telling of his response to it.

She hadn't particularly meant to insult the man, but it was nevertheless true that he didn't appear to have a forthright bone in his body. 'I'll go and make that appointment,' she said quickly. 'Er—thank you for your help,' she added, with the gratitude she had omitted earlier.

It started out as that now-familiar grimace, but then it went one step further, and, to her surprise, Brianna found herself looking at a smiling Nathan Landris. It was quite amazing what a difference it made to him—his blue eyes warm, that hard, unyielding face suddenly rakishly attractive.

Brianna stared at him, totally thrown by the transformation. God, this man had it all, didn't he: a razor-sharp brain, a lethal coldness, and, when that failed, a sudden charm that was breathtaking. At least, Brianna felt suddenly breathless. Clark Kent and Superman—and she had thought they were both ficticious characters!

'I think so.' He answered her facetiously made remark. 'You speak first, and think afterwards.'

'Whereas a lawyer thinks first and often doesn't speak at all.' She acknowledged the fact that, although he might think he had almost told her his life story, he had in fact told her nothing she had come here to find out. And she was no longer sure that was because he didn't know anything... 'Very well, Mr Landris, we'll do this your way.' She doubted it was very often done any other way! 'You escort me back to Reception, I'll organise my appointment, and then we can both get back to work.'

He walked at her side down the corridor, the glasses firmly back on the bridge of his nose. 'And what work do you do, Miss Gibson?'

She glanced up at him, tongue slightly in cheek as she answered him. 'I'm a receptionist.'

This time the smile that closely resembled a grimace didn't even get a look in. That rakish grin appeared instantly, accompanied by a throaty chuckle. 'Miss Gib—Brianna, you really are...!' He shook his head, the grin still curving his lips. 'I don't think you need any assistance in organising your appointment. I—' He broke off, looking at a man walking down the corridor toward them, and his humour faded, his expression suddenly becoming grim.

'Can you find your own way back to Reception?' he prompted Brianna distractedly, still looking at the other man.

'I would think so,' she answered him humorously, also looking at the man approaching them. He was dressed as formally as Nathan Landris but he wasn't quite as tall as him, although he had an equal air of purpose about him. Nathan Landris's two o'clock appointment, Brianna decided.

'Could you wait in my office for me?' Nathan addressed the man, confirming Brianna's suspicions. 'I'll be with you in a moment.'

'I'm in rather a hurry, Nathan,' the older man said sharply.

'This won't take long,' Nathan assured him.

'I can see you're busy.' Brianna lightly touched Nathan's arm. 'I won't take up any more of your time.' She gave an apologetic smile to the older man—who, despite being much older than Nathan, *did* give her a male response, openly staring at her.

Brianna's parting smile included both men as she walked away, and as she glanced back, before turning the corner into the reception area, it was to find both men still watching her, the older still staring at her. Nathan Landris might be made of ice, but his client certainly wasn't!

Brianna, out on the street minutes later, her appointment made for next week with Landris Senior, felt distinctly dissatisfied with the whole morning; she was no nearer to knowing what all this was about than she had been when she'd received the letter earlier that day!

CHAPTER TWO

'YOU really shouldn't have gone there alone, Brianna.' Her father spoke across the dinner table to her. 'I thought we agreed before you left for work this morning that you weren't going to do anything until we had another chance to talk this evening?'

'Don't worry, Dad.' Brianna leant across the table and squeezed his hand reassuringly. 'For all the good it did me, I might as well not have bothered! I feel as if I just made a complete fool of myself.' And Nathan Landris had helped her to do it!

She had thought on and off during the afternoon about her conversation with him; the more she thought about it, the more annoyed she became, both with him and herself. Who had been trying to glean information from whom?

'I think it's ace,' her brother piped up. 'Perhaps you'll find out you're the daughter of a rich Arab sheik, and that you've been left millions in his will!' Gary grinned expectantly.

As a family, they had never made any secret of Brianna's adoption, and, because they were all so close, it had never mattered to any of them—Gary was Brianna's brother, and her father was exactly that.

She grimaced now. 'With this colouring? Knowing my luck, it's more likely I'm the daughter of a debtor—and I owe millions!'

Her brother grinned, she noticed, but her father still looked far from happy with the situation. 'Dad—' She broke off as the telephone rang out in the hallway. 'You aren't on call tonight, are you?' She frowned.

'No, I'm not. But when has that ever stopped patients calling me?'

Her father specialised in obstetrics, and as such was always on call!

'I'll get it,' Gary offered, getting up from the table.

'It's probably for you, anyway,' Brianna said; her brother seemed to have a veritable stream of girlfriends.

'Or the rich Arab sheik for you!' he called out cheekily before leaving the room.

'Not if he's dead!' she returned lightly.

'We're all so normal.' Her father slowly shook his head. 'Just a normal happy family. And yet I have this strong feeling of impending doom, like a heavy weight hanging over us all. I—'

'It's for you, sis.' Gary breezed back into the room. 'A Mr Landris.'

'You see.' Her father sat back heavily, looking every inch his fifty-three years at that moment.

Nathan Landris! What on earth was he telephoning her for, at home, at seven o'clock in the evening? Unless he was a workaholic, it was way out of office hours. Come to think of it, he probably was a workaholic! But she didn't have any business with him; it was his father she wanted to see. Surely this wasn't a social call? Superman hadn't burst out of Clark Kent's clothing, had he, with Nathan Landris actually behaving like a man rather than a lawyer? No, it was the Incredible Hulk who burst out of his clothes, not Superman—

'I don't think he's going to hang on all evening, Bri,' Gary urged. 'He sounded a bit pompous to me.'

Nathan Landris, the Ice Man, Brianna decided ruefully as she stood up, lightly touching her father on the shoulder as she passed him. 'It will be okay, Dad,' she assured him huskily. 'You'll see.'

'I hope so.' He still looked haggard. 'I don't want to lose you, Brianna.'

'You won't,' she told him firmly, before going out into the hallway to take the call, picking up the telephone receiver. 'Nathan,' she greeted coolly. 'To what do I owe the pleasure of this call?' She started the conversation in the way she meant it to continue!

There was a moment's pause on the other end of the line before an answer came. 'It is a pleasure to speak to you, Miss Gibson, but I'm afraid this isn't Nathan,' said a male voice she didn't recognise. 'My name is Peter Landris. I'm Nathan's father.'

She had realised it wasn't Nathan the moment he spoke. Oh, the accent was just as refined, the voice almost as deep, but it certainly wasn't Nathan. 'I'm so sorry, Mr Landris.' She gave an inward grimace at her *faux pas*. 'I—'

'Please don't be,' he returned smoothly. 'It was a natural mistake for you to have made, in the circumstances.'

What circumstances? She was even more stunned now that she knew her caller was Landris Senior!

'I understand that you spoke with my son earlier today,' Peter Landris continued lightly, as if aware of her confusion and giving her time to recover.

Those circumstances. 'Yes, I did.' Now she couldn't help wondering exactly what his son had said about their meeting! 'He explained you were unavailable,' she added pointedly; he obviously wasn't unavailable this evening!

'That's the reason I'm calling, actually,' he came back calmly. 'I realise you have made an appointment to see me next week, but I find I have a window in my schedule tomorrow, at one o'clock, and wondered if you would like to come in and see me then instead?'

If she took a late lunch, and wasn't gone too long... 'Could you make it one-fifteen?' She wasn't sure how wide this window was!

'I'm sure I can,' he accepted briskly. 'One-fifteen tomorrow, then, Miss Gibson.' He abruptly ended the call.

Brianna quickly put down her own receiver. Not quite the Ice Man, but it was obvious where Nathan had learnt his terseness; the reason for the call was concluded, and so was the call itself!

What a strange family the Landrises were, Brianna decided, shaking her head ruefully. But she had an appointment to see Peter Landris, and it wasn't for next week, either. Now all she had to do was go back to the dining-room and reassure her father...

Brianna sat across from Peter Landris, his desk between them. He was the man who had been walking down the corridor yesterday, as she was leaving, the man Nathan had asked to wait for him in his office—the man she had assumed was Nathan's two o'clock appointment.

Peter Landris was the man whom Nathan had known she'd come here to see yesterday—and to whom she was sure he had deliberately chosen not to introduce her!

Her eyes sparkled deeply blue as she looked across the desk at the elder Landris. As she knew from yesterday, he was slightly shorter than his son, although he probably still reached six feet, and with the knowledge of their relationship she was now able to see the similarities between the two men. Both were dark-haired, although Peter Landris's hair was liberally peppered with grey, and they both had those strongly hewn faces, dominated by cold, pale blue eyes. In fact, Peter Landris was looking at her very much as his son had done yesterday!

Brianna bristled resentfully. The Landris family, with their initial letter sent to her father three months ago, and the one sent directly to her yesterday, had already wreaked havoc in her previously harmonious life; she was the one who should be angry. And she was!

'You wanted to see me, Mr Landris?' she prompted. 'This is my lunch hour and I really don't have a lot of time.'

To her surprise, he smiled, and, as with his son, it changed his whole demeanour, giving warmth to his eyes and a boyish charm to those hard features. Brianna decided at that moment that she wouldn't like to face either father or son in a court-room—their charm would be totally disconcerting, before the coldness ripped you to shreds!

'It's my lunchbreak too,' he told her softly. 'Perhaps I should order us some coffee and sandwiches?'

Her expression deepened. 'Am I going to be here long enough to eat them?' She had imagined this meeting wouldn't take long at all!

His smile broadened as he picked up the telephone. 'Nathan told me you're extremely direct,' he murmured, before talking briskly into the receiver. 'Hazel—coffee and sandwiches for Miss Gibson and myself. Thank you.' He ended the call as abruptly as he had with Brianna the evening before.

'I can't see the point of being any other way.' Brianna answered his previous statement—although she could imagine all too well what Nathan had told his father about her. But, unlike poor Hazel, she had no reason to be in awe of either man. And she wasn't. 'I dislike mysteries, Mr Landris, and this has certainly become one.'

She no longer believed a mistake had been made concerning her identity; this man didn't make those kind of mistakes! And if it wasn't an error, then she wanted to know as quickly as possible what it was all about.

'I'm sorry if you feel that way,' Peter Landris returned politely. 'It certainly wasn't meant to be.'

'Exactly what is "it", Mr Landris?' Brianna prompted impatiently.

'There are certain formalities to get through before I— Ah, Hazel.' He turned to the receptionist as she came in with a laden tray, moving several papers aside on his desk to make room for the woman to put it down. 'Would you like to pour?' he invited Brianna, once the receptionist had departed.

'No, I do not want to pour!' Brianna burst out irritably; they were never going to get to the point of the meeting at this rate! 'Mr Landris— Oh good grief!' she snapped, as there was a brief knock on the outer door before Nathan walked into the room. 'This is worse than Piccadilly Circus in the rush hour!' she muttered.

Although if she was annoyed at yet another interruption, then Nathan looked absolutely stunned to see her sitting in his father's office. Which meant he couldn't have known of his father's telephone call to her last night...

'Nathan,' his father greeted without warmth. 'As you can see, I'm busy,' he added pointedly.

The younger man didn't move. 'You didn't tell me you intended seeing Brianna today.'

His father reacted to what sounded like an accusation. 'I don't believe it's something I have to inform you of, Nathan,' he rasped.

'And I don't believe you introduced me to your father yesterday, either, Nathan,' Brianna interrupted. Father and son seemed to be locked in a silent battle with each other, so much so that she, the apparent reason for the tension between them, was briefly forgotten.

Nathan glanced at her momentarily before turning to his father. 'Perhaps we could talk in private for a few minutes,' he bit out harshly. 'In my office,' he added determinedly.

His father didn't so much as move a muscle. 'I don't think so, Nathan.'

'Father, I really think—'

'I told you, no, Nathan,' his father said glacially. 'Now, if you wouldn't mind, I'm in the middle of a confidential meeting with my client.'

Brianna turned to him sharply. Client? She most certainly was not a client of his. For one thing, clients deliberately sought out the services of lawyers, something she most certainly had not done where Peter Landris and his son were concerned. And, for another, she could never have afforded the prices of a prestigious firm like this one, so if either of them had the least idea of presenting her with a bill for these two meetings, they could just think again…!

She stood up, picking up her handbag. 'I'll leave the two of you to sort out your differences. And then, when you have, perhaps you would like to send me a letter stating exactly what all this is about, Mr Landris,' she suggested to the older man. After all, he was the one who had just claimed she was a client! 'I really don't have any more time to waste today,' she added.

'You were right, Nathan.' Peter Landris spoke quietly as she crossed the room. 'Brianna is as wilful as her mother.'

Brianna stopped, feeling the colour drain from her cheeks as she slowly turned to face him. 'My mother?' she repeated slowly, her lips suddenly feeling so stiff she could barely speak. 'You know my mother?'

'Yes. Nathan, help Brianna back to her chair before she falls down,' Peter Landris added calmly, as she swayed on her feet.

She was barely aware of the arm about her waist, of being guided back to the chair she had so recently vacated, of sitting down. She could only stare at Peter Landris with suddenly very dark blue eyes. 'You're talking about my biological mother?' she asked weakly. Having her father suspect that this was the reason for the letters was one thing; it was quite another for it to turn out to be true!

'Of course,' Peter Landris answered briskly, taking a file out of the top drawer of his desk. 'I would—'

'Father!' Nathan barked tensely. 'There are papers to see first, to be verified—'

'Nathan, I will not tell you again!' his father returned forcefully, eyes glacially blue. 'Do not attempt to tell me how to do my job. I am well aware of what has to be done. But Rebecca was my client, and now that makes Brianna so.'

'Rebecca is my mother?' Brianna wasn't in the least interested in the argument between father and son; in fact the more she heard the less sure she was that she wanted to know about any of it. Her mother had been Jean Gibson—she was the person who had cared for Brianna as a helpless baby, who had cuddled her when she hurt herself, who had wept for her on the day she began school, helped to ease the pain of her first broken love affair, sat and talked to her in the night when she panicked about her exams, had been pleased for her when she secured the job she wanted. Jean was her mother. She didn't even want to know that this other woman's name was Rebecca—suddenly felt as if the life she had always known was being invaded, violated...

'She was,' Peter Landris confirmed in a gentle voice.

Brianna swallowed hard. Was...? 'She's dead?'

'I'm afraid so, my dear,' he said. 'Rebecca—'

'I don't want to know!' she cut in emotionally. And she didn't. She had wanted this meeting, the reason for it, out of the way, so that she could forget about it and get on with her life. But now she had a feeling that once she had heard the truth her life would be changed for ever. She didn't want that.

'I don't want to know,' she repeated flatly as the two men looked at her. 'Whoever this woman Rebecca was, whatever she was, she most certainly was not my mother.' She felt no loss at knowing of Rebecca's death. How could she? She had never known the lady. And now that Rebecca was dead, there was no reason for her to know that, either. 'Whatever this is about,' she told Peter tersely, 'I want no part of it.'

'It isn't as easy at that, Brianna—'

'It most certainly is,' she interrupted the older man firmly. 'My mother abandoned me, gave me up; I now have the right to do the same where she's concerned.' She looked at him challengingly.

'You're oversimplifying things, Brianna—'

'I most certainly am not,' she replied strongly, feeling her self-determination returning rapidly. She had been thrown for a few minutes, but now she was in control again. 'If a parent can choose to abandon a child, then that child can choose to abandon the parent.'

'Nathan, will you either come into the room or get out of it.' Peter Landris spoke sharply to his son as a young woman walked by along the corridor outside. 'This is an intensely personal matter; I do not want all and sundry to hear about it!'

'I'm well aware of how private it is,' Nathan told him icily, moving further into the room and shutting the door firmly behind him.

His father looked at him intently. 'Exactly what do you mean by that remark?'

The younger man gave him a scathing glance. 'Exactly what I said,' he snapped back, before turning his attention to Brianna. 'I think you should listen to my father, Brianna,' he told her harshly. 'You stand to be a very wealthy woman at the end of this conversation!'

She gave him a pitying look. He was neither Clark Kent nor Superman; he couldn't even see that wealth didn't interest her in the least. Maybe it was because he obviously came from such a well-off family himself that he just couldn't imagine anyone being happy without money!

'I'm not interested,' she told the elder Landris firmly. 'I have a family already; I don't need to know of another one.'

He raised dark brows; she was clearly adamant. 'I understand your adoptive mother is dead.'

'What does that have to do with this?' Brianna bristled indignantly, eyes sparkling angrily, not even interested as to how he knew of Jean's death. 'It appears that both my adoptive mother and my biological mother are dead—I can assure you I know which one I mourn! This other woman—Rebecca—means nothing to me. And neither does any money she may have left me. She didn't care about me enough over the last twenty-one years to seek me out, so I have no intention of her recent death intruding on my life now!' She was breathing hard in her agitation.

'But your mother didn't die recently, Brianna,' Peter Landris told her quietly. 'She died twenty-one years ago.'

Brianna blinked at him, totally speechless. She had never really thought of her real mother as she grew up, had been totally secure in the love of her adoptive parents. Even once she had reached adulthood it had never occurred to her to seek out the woman who had given birth to her. She had accepted that the woman probably had—probably still had—a life that wouldn't welcome the daughter she had given birth to years ago. Somehow she had never imagined that her biological mother might have died so long ago...

She moistened her lips. 'How did she die?'

'The cause of death on the death certificate?' Peter Landris returned hardly.

She frowned at him, at the way he had voiced the question. She knew all about death certificates—as a doctor, sadly her father had occasionally had to sign them—but from the way Peter Landris spoke there was clearly some doubt about her mother's—Rebecca's...

'It's usually pretty accurate,' she said flatly.

'Not in this case,' Peter Landris countered. 'The last I heard, they didn't list a broken heart as the cause of death,' he added bitterly.

'Father, you're too close to this,' Nathan put in, stepping forward. 'Too involved. Worse than that, you're alarming Brianna.'

She wasn't alarmed; she was confused. Just exactly when had her mother died twenty-one years ago? Obviously some time soon after Brianna's arrival. But if she had died because of the birth of her baby, why hadn't Brianna been taken in by relatives rather than put up for adoption. Who were her real family?

Peter Landris drew in a deeply controlling breath. 'I'm sorry, Brianna. I just— It's the waste!' He shook his head, his face pale. 'I was never able to accept the ending of that beautiful life. The utter futility of it all. You're right, Nathan, I thought I could deal with this, but I—' He gave a shaky sigh. 'Seeing Brianna has brought it all back to me.' He looked across the desk at her. 'You look so much like— God, it's unnerving!'

She looked like her mother... Like Rebecca...? And, from this man's behaviour now, he had known her real mother very well...

Her mouth tightened. 'Who was my father?'

Peter Landris grimaced. 'Your mother refused to name your father.'

Brianna shook her head. 'I find it hard to believe that no one knew.'

'You wouldn't if you'd known Giles,' Peter Landris rasped with feeling.

'Who was Giles?' She sighed her impatience with this disjointed conversation. This was becoming more and more complicated by the moment!

'Your grandfather. Rebecca's father,' Nathan told her without hesitation. 'Rebecca was terrified of him.'

Brianna turned to him with shadowed blue eyes. 'You knew my mother too?' Twenty-one years ago Nathan would only have been fourteen!

'I did,' he confirmed curtly. 'She was four years older than me, but—'

'My mother—Rebecca,' she corrected herself, 'was only eighteen when she gave birth to me?' No more than a child herself! 'And when she died...' Brianna realised dazedly. She had been far too young to die. And yet Rebecca had loved, and apparently lost, and had given birth to Brianna in those brief eighteen years...

'I'm afraid this interview isn't being carried out very professionally.' Nathan gave his father a reproving look. 'Ordinarily, in these circumstances, we would ask you for documentary proof of who you are. And then—'

'She's Rebecca's daughter.' Peter Landris was staring at her now as if he was seeing a ghost. 'Without a shadow of a doubt!'

'I agree with you,' Nathan concurred. 'I knew that the moment I saw her in Reception yesterday.'

'You could have told me!' Brianna snapped angrily. 'Instead of which you carried out some sort of elaborate delaying charade. This all happened twenty-one years ago, isn't that delay enough?' she bit out accusingly, looking from one man to the other to emphasise the point that she was tired of this further prevarication. She wanted the facts, and she wanted them now. There would be time later, once she was alone, to sit and brood over the significance—or otherwise!—of them to her life now. 'Nathan?' she pressed. 'You seem to know all about this, so you tell me what happened all those years ago!' The need to return to work was right at the bottom of her priorities now!

'Rebecca was *my* client—'

'Rebecca is dead,' Brianna coldly cut into Peter Landris's protest. 'I appear to be your client now—and I would rather hear this from Nathan.' He, at least, appeared able to talk about all of this unemotionally.

'Father?' Nathan glanced at the older man.

'Go ahead,' his father invited dully. 'I— Seeing Brianna, the likeness to— It's been a shock...'

'Have a cup of cold coffee and a rapidly curling sandwich.' Brianna poured the coffee for him, before turning back to the younger man. 'Nathan?' she pressed again, his father forgotten.

Nathan sighed, pulling up another chair and sitting down on the same side of the desk as Brianna, his pale blue eyes strangely compassionate. 'We have to start with your grandparents—'

'Rebecca's mother and father?'

'This will be much quicker if you don't interrupt after every statement,' Nathan told her sharply.

Much quicker. Although she had pushed the need to

return to work firmly to the back of her mind, time was still passing rapidly. 'Sorry,' she ventured.

He acknowledged her apology with an arrogant nod of his head. 'Your grandparents—Joanne and Giles. Joanne was the daughter of a very rich man; Giles was a local farmer. But, nevertheless, the two of them apparently fell in love and married. A year into the marriage Joanne gave birth to Rebecca. There were to be no more children.'

This was much better, much easier for Brianna to deal with emotionally.

'Despite its apparently romantic beginning—' Nathan couldn't seem to help the cynical twist to his lips that accompanied this statement '—it wasn't a particularly happy marriage. Giles came to quickly resent the fact that it was his wife who held the purse-strings, and he didn't care for his daughter, or the pull she had on her mother's time and love.'

'It should have read "broken heart" on Joanne's death certificate too,' Peter Landris muttered harshly.

Nathan glared his father into silence. 'At the age of eight, Rebecca was sent away to boarding-school,' he continued evenly. 'Her mother, it seems, never got over the loss.'

'But there must have been holidays—'

'Giles always made sure they were out of the country for those.' It was Peter Landris who answered her. 'Leaving Rebecca in the care of a housekeeper when she was at home. Joanne rarely saw her daughter during the next three years.'

'I— But that's inhuman!' Brianna protested. 'How could anyone be so cruel?'

'If I could just continue?' Nathan cut in icily, his brows raised as he waited for Brianna's attention to return to him.

'But this is all so—it's like something out of a Victorian novel.' Brianna shook her head dazedly. 'I can't believe anyone could get away with treating his wife and daughter in that way less than forty years ago!'

'Can't you?' Nathan said bleakly. 'Then perhaps you should see some of the cases that come to court nowadays!'

She had seen some of the battered wives and children that were brought into the hospital. 'But Joanne was the one with the money.' She frowned. 'Surely that gave her a certain amount of—freedom?'

'Giles was Rebecca's father—a fact he never let Joanne forget,' Peter Landris put in baldly. 'I can assure you, Joanne was by no means a weak woman, but she did have a weakness. And that weakness was her child.'

Not physical cruelty, Brianna realised, but emotional blackmail—who could say which was worse?

'Go on,' she invited gruffly, wondering what other horrors she was going to hear about her family; perhaps Rebecca had done her the biggest favour of all by keeping her well away from them!

'When Rebecca was thirteen, her mother died.' Nathan was now the one to continue. He shot his father another censorious look as he added, 'In a car accident. But her death left Rebecca with only her father.'

'He didn't take her out of boarding-school?' Brianna said worriedly, beginning to care about Rebecca in spite of herself. Her own childhood had been such a happy one, with parents and a brother who loved her, she simply couldn't bear the thought of the loneliness Rebecca must have endured as she was growing up.

'No, he didn't do that.' Nathan gave the ghost of a smile in reassurance. 'Rebecca continued to stay at the boarding-school; her father continued to be absent when she came home for the holidays. But there were no letters or telephone calls from her mother to sustain her. As was to be expected, Rebecca became desperate for love, for someone to care about her. As she got older there were—relationships. The majority of them with totally unsuitable men. But in this Giles had no say. What could he have threatened Rebecca with?' Nathan stated frankly. 'He had never given her anything he could possibly take away from her.'

Brianna was watching Nathan closely, questioningly. 'You liked my mother,' she said slowly, realising there was a warmth in his voice as he spoke of her.

Emotion flashed briefly in those pale blue eyes behind the glasses, and then it was gone, replaced by that mask of professionalism she was used to. 'Rebecca, despite her unorthodox upbringing, was impossible not to like. She was full of life, and laughter, and beauty. Perhaps too much of the latter,' he added wistfully. 'It left her prey to the—attentions of men.'

Brianna frowned. 'Are you saying my mother was promiscuous?'

'Certainly not,' he snapped, his mouth a thin line. 'I'm saying she didn't always love wisely.'

'As she didn't where my father was concerned. Did he happen to be married to someone else?' Brianna guessed shrewdly.

'We don't know,' Nathan said flatly. 'Perhaps.' He shrugged those broad shoulders. 'Perhaps her letter to you will explain all that to you,' he added gruffly, glancing briefly at his father.

Brianna looked at him sharply, disbelievingly. She had learnt so much of Rebecca's background in the last few minutes. Her father, she believed, had been a despot who denied his wife and daughter their love for each other. Rebecca had been the emotionally deprived child of that union, a child who had grown to young womanhood craving love, and not always finding it in the places that she should have.

Brianna had listened to all of this, had felt pity for her grandmother and her mother in an abstract way, even a little for the grandfather who must have been a very insecure man to have ruled his family in the way that he had. She had listened and had felt sorrow for such unhappiness, but it was a story of someone else's life—a life unrelated to her own.

But a letter... A letter written to her by her mother was so much more...

She didn't want it.

Didn't want it.

Couldn't read it...

CHAPTER THREE

'GENTLEMEN.' She stood up. 'I thank you for your time, and the information you've given me today. Now I have more of an idea of what my natural mother and her family were like.' She turned to leave.

'Where are you going?' Pete Landris sounded bewildered by her dismissal.

She turned back only slightly. 'I have to get back to work now.'

'But—'

'I'll drive you.' Nathan had moved silently to her side.

'But we haven't finished,' his father protested behind them. 'There's so much more. Rebecca's death. Brianna's inheritance—'

'And Brianna has had more than enough already today for her to cope with,' Nathan told him harshly, before turning back to Brianna. 'I'll drive you wherever you want to go,' he offered gently.

'I'm sure you're very busy,' she refused vaguely, needing to be away from these offices, away from the two Landris men. 'I can get a bus. Take a taxi.'

'I'm not busy at all,' Nathan said firmly, lightly grasping her arm as they went out into the corridor. 'The buses are incredibly irregular around here. And a taxi would be an unnecessary expense when I've already offered to drive you wherever you want to go.'

Brianna didn't argue any more, standing silently by while Nathan informed Hazel of his departure, taking no interest in the brief conversation he had with a grey-haired man passing through Reception, although she

sensed the other man's interest in her as she left with
Nathan. Not another one who recognised her as
Rebecca's daughter…! It was a very strange feeling to
know she looked so much like someone she had never
even known—and would never know…

'My uncle, Roger Davis,' Nathan supplied as he took
her out to the private car park at the back of the building.
'He's married to my mother's sister.'

He was also Nathan's father's partner. It really was a
family-run business. And the Landris family seemed to
know rather a lot about her mother and *her* family. Too
much so, in the circumstances, Brianna was beginning
to realise. 'Nathan—'

'Here we are.' He unlocked a dark green Jaguar sa-
loon car, opening the passenger door for Brianna to get
in. 'Just tell me where you want to go,' he said, once
he was seated beside her.

She gave him the name of the hospital where she
worked, watching him as he drove. He handled the car
in the same way he seemed to deal with everything,
capably, with the minimum of effort, and completely
unemotionally—even when another driver cut dangerously in front of the Jaguar at a busy junction. The Ice
Man, no matter what the situation.

'Have dinner with me this evening?'

His invitation was so at odds with her thoughts of him
that for a moment Brianna was stunned into silence. The
icy Nathan Landris had just invited her out to dinner
with him!

'Why?' she returned abruptly.

Dark brows rose over those pale blue eyes, his mouth
quirking, although his visual attention didn't waver from
the road and traffic in front of him. 'Is this your usual
response when a man invites you to spend the evening
with him?'

Her mouth curved upwards, some of her earlier tension leaving her. 'No,' she acknowledged. 'But then, it wasn't a usual invitation!'

'I can assure you that it was,' he drawled.

Her eyes widened. 'It was?'

'It was,' he confirmed dryly. 'Unless there's a young man in your life somewhere whom you feel might object to your accepting?'

Brianna had the feeling the question wasn't as casually asked as he'd made it sound. Although why he should have any interest in the romantic side of her life, she couldn't imagine. Even if he had invited her out to dinner...

'Not at the moment, no,' she answered him smilingly.

Her most recent relationship, with a young doctor at the hospital, had ended three months ago, by mutual agreement; Jim had worked nights and Brianna had worked days, and the strain of trying to keep up even a casual relationship had finally proved too much of a strain.

'Then I repeat, would you have dinner with me this evening?' Nathan pressed her.

In her head she repeated her own question—why? Nathan didn't give her the impression he was in the least impulsive—in fact quite the opposite!—and, despite what he said, she didn't think this invitation was unpremeditated, either.

Nathan turned and smiled at her, the smile that transformed him from a coldly removed man to a rakishly charming one, as she had glimpsed yesterday. A dangerously attractive one...! He couldn't be two people, and yet...

'Is there a young lady in your life who might object to my accepting?' she returned evenly.

His mouth quirked again. 'Not at the moment, no.' He repeated her words of a few minutes ago.

It was the answer Brianna had expected him to make. Not because she didn't think there hadn't been women in his life—that smile said otherwise!—but because she didn't think he was the type of man to invite one woman out while he was involved with another. For one thing, she doubted he would want the complications that would involve.

'In that case, I accept,' she told him.

He nodded, showing no emotion at her capitulation. 'I'll call at your home for you, at eight o'clock. I have the address.' He forestalled her next comment. 'It's on file at the office.'

Of course it was. As were a lot of other things, things personal to her, things that, until today, she'd had had no knowledge of. Most of which she would rather still have no knowledge of, including a letter Rebecca seemed to have left for her!

The puzzle of that letter was going to burn a hole in her curiosity; she knew it was. Already part of her was wondering what was written there, what her mother had wanted to say to her daughter once she reached twenty-one. Had Rebecca loved her baby? Hated her because she had complicated her life? Did she say who Brianna's father was? Had she even known who he was?

Did it matter? Did any of it matter? It was the past, the principal player dead and buried long ago—

'He's still alive, you know.' Nathan spoke softly at her side.

She gave him a startled look. 'Who is?' She was completely taken aback, both because he seemed to have read her thoughts so easily, and by the statement itself. He had stated earlier that her mother hadn't said who her father was, that no one knew—

'Your grandfather,' Nathan said in reply. 'Giles is still alive.'

Brianna looked at him uncomprehendingly for several long seconds. That man, the man who had made her grandmother's and her mother's lives such a misery, was still living? It didn't seem fair somehow, not after all the misery he had caused to his family.

'Did you hear me, Brianna?' Nathan glanced at her frowningly. 'I said—'

'I heard you,' she said tensely, surprised—and pleased!—to see that they had arrived at the hospital. 'Thank you for the lift, Nathan.' She gave him a bright, meaningless smile. 'I'll see you later this evening.'

The engine switched off, he turned in his seat towards her, one of his hands reaching out to clasp both of hers. 'It will get easier, Brianna,' he assured her. 'Once the shock of all this wears off.'

'If it ever does.' She gave a self-derisive laugh. 'I feel as if I've been dragged into a Victorian novel, totally out of time, and out of my depth because everyone else knows the plot! And, talking of time—' she gave a hasty look at her wristwatch '—I'm at least half an hour late back from lunch already.' Her colleague, left holding the fort on her own, wouldn't appreciate that.

Nathan removed his hand from hers. 'I'll see you at eight o'clock tonight.'

Brianna didn't glance back at the Jaguar as she hurried up the hospital steps, even though she knew the car, and its driver, hadn't left yet. Nathan might have removed his hand from hers, but she could still feel its warmth, the imprint of those long, slender fingers against hers. Finding herself attracted to Nathan Landris was a complication she just didn't need at the moment. She had enough to cope with already!

*　　*　　*

'He sounds awful.' Brianna's father looked perturbed after she had given him a description of Rebecca's father.

'Doesn't he just!' Brianna agreed, sitting in the kitchen enjoying a cup of coffee with her father after having served his evening meal to him. Gary had, as usual, eaten his dinner quickly and gone out again. 'The sort of man you could cheerfully punch on the nose and walk away from without a moment's regret!' Back in the normality of her own family, the time spent in Peter Landris's office earlier today seemed to have taken on a dream-like quality. Her maternal grandfather didn't just sound like a despot, he sounded unreal!

Her father looked at her closely. 'Does that mean you intend going to see him?'

'Certainly not!' She laughed dismissively. 'He may have cowed Joanne and Rebecca, but he wouldn't have the same success with me. Much better to leave the old curmudgeon to his bitterness.' She pulled a face. 'I think the whole episode is better left in the past, where it belongs.'

She had told her father almost everything about the meeting in Peter Landris's office. Except about the letter. She felt guilty about the omission, but at the same time it was something she didn't want to talk about, because she was still unresolved in her own mind as to what to do about it. Her father, she knew, despite his own reluctance for the past to intrude into their lives, would feel she should at least read Rebecca's letter...

'And yet you're having dinner with Nathan Landris this evening?' Her father looked puzzled now, Brianna having explained this was the reason why she hadn't eaten with him and Gary.

She could feel the blush in her cheeks. 'I— That has nothing to do with this.' In her mind, it didn't. Nathan was an enigma, and, in spite of herself, he intrigued her.

Her father frowned. 'Then what *does* it have to do with? I can't see the two of you spending the evening together without the subject of your natural mother entering into the conversation.' He shook his head.

Brianna gave him a cheeky grin as she stood up. 'I can!' She leant down and gave him an affectionate kiss on the cheek. 'Don't wait up for me, Dad—I could be late!'

But, despite her bravado with her father, she was a little uncertain herself how this evening with Nathan would turn out. After all, as far as she was aware, they had nothing in common but this business concerning her mother, and as she had no intention of talking about that, it could be a very quiet—and short-lived!—meal.

But she needn't have worried; Nathan didn't seem to want to pursue the subject either, and he turned out to be a very knowledgeable conversationalist. The two of them quickly discovered a mutual interest in golf, a game that Brianna often played with her father at the weekends, and Nathan told her about some of the funnier incidents he had encountered while playing the game.

'We'll have to play a round together some time.'

Brianna had been so intent on watching him as he talked, rather than actually listening to what he was saying, that it took her a few seconds for this last comment to sink in. And, when it did, the blush of earlier that day returned to her cheeks.

Nathan gave a rueful shake of his head. 'I wondered if that might get your attention,' he mused dryly. 'You weren't listening to a word I said, were you?' He raised those quizzical dark brows.

It was his own fault that her thoughts had been so far away. He'd looked tall and distinguished in the suits he wore for work, but, even so, she had been completely unprepared for the way he looked in a black dinner suit

and snowy white shirt, his hair still damp from the
shower he must have taken, when he had arrived at her
home for her a short time ago. And he wasn't wearing
his black-rimmed glasses this evening, either, revealing
to Brianna the ridiculously long dark lashes that framed
his pale blue eyes. Superman…!

'I was just wondering what had happened to your
glasses this evening,' she blurted out inconsequentially;
she could hardly tell him what she had really been thinking!

'Were you?' he teased—as if he knew damn well she
hadn't been thinking about anything of the sort! 'I only
need to wear them for reading,' he explained.

'And driving.' She remembered he had been wearing
them earlier when he drove her back to the hospital. She
wished he was wearing them now, too; he was far less
approachable in those spectacles. And she was quickly
discovering she needed him to be unapproachable!

He grimaced. 'Er—actually, no.'

'But—'

'I forgot to take them off when I left the office with
you this afternoon,' he admitted.

So he had been as disturbed by the meeting in his
father's office as she had! She wondered why. After all,
despite the fact that Nathan and his father had seemed
to know Rebecca, only Giles appeared to be left, and
neither Landris approved of him!

Brianna grinned; her hair was soft on her shoulders
and she was wearing a fitted black dress, its short length
showing off her long, shapely legs. She had been glad,
once they'd reached this expensively discreet restaurant,
that she had dressed for the evening. Somehow she had
known Nathan didn't intend taking her to a local fast
food restaurant!

'I would love to play a round of gold with you some

time,' she told him. 'Although I should warn you, my father has been taking me out with him since I was big enough to hold a club!' Golf was her father's passion, a way of relaxing after a hard day with his patients.

'In that case, perhaps we should invite your father to join us; I would hate to deprive him of his golfing partner.' Nathan smiled warmly.

Brianna held back. The two men had met briefly earlier, when Nathan called to collect her, but it wasn't an acquaintance Brianna felt her father wanted to deepen; his manner earlier had been uncharacteristically stiff and formal. Not that she could exactly blame him for feeling that way; the Landris family were intruding into the life he had created for his own family.

'My father is a very busy man.'

'And he doesn't like me,' Nathan guessed easily.

'It isn't that,' Brianna began awkwardly.

'I wasn't criticising, Brianna.' Nathan's hand briefly covered hers on the table-top. 'In the same circumstances *I* wouldn't want me near my daughter either!'

She laughed. 'That was a little grammatically incorrect—but I get your meaning!'

Now Nathan was the one to stare at her, those pale blue eyes no longer in the least icy. 'You know, Brianna,' he said slowly 'when you laugh—'

'I look exactly like Rebecca,' she finished quickly. This was ridiculous; she was starting to feel jealous of a woman who had died over twenty years ago! No...not jealous, exactly, it was just that Rebecca seemed to have made such an impact on the men that she'd come into contact with. Nathan included...

'I wasn't about to say that at all,' Nathan bit out, removing his hand from hers, dark brows settling low over narrowed eyes.

'No?' she challenged sceptically.

'No!' His eyes glittered ominously. 'You—' He broke off abruptly as the food they had ordered earlier arrived, stony-faced as the waiter put their plates on the table in front of them. 'Let's get one thing clear, Brianna.' Nathan leant forward to mutter to her once they were alone again. 'Our having dinner together has nothing whatsoever to do with your mother. In fact, I would prefer it if you weren't Rebecca's daughter. But you are, so that preference is a non-starter. I would, however, rather not talk about her.'

Brianna met his gaze rebelliously, her eyes sparkling brightly. 'That suits me just fine!'

'Good,' he snapped, attacking the prawns on his plate as if they were the reason for his annoyance.

Brianna watched him for several seconds, her resentment slowly fading, her humour returning. 'Nathan,' she finally said, smiling as he scowled across at her, 'relax and enjoy your meal; those poor prawns have done nothing to you!' she teased. 'Besides, I don't know about you, but I had no lunch today and I'm starving!'

He glared at her irritably for a moment, and then the tension went out of his shoulders as he took her advice and began to relax. 'You're an infuriating woman, Brianna Gibson,' he finally muttered, shaking his head.

'That's good.' She grinned as he looked at her enquiringly. 'I'd rather be infuriating than insipid!' she explained.

He raised his eyes heavenwards. 'Don't worry, that's one insult that will never be levelled at you by me!'

'But there'll be plenty of others, hmm?' she said knowingly, eating her pâté with enjoyment.

'Probably,' he replied tersely.

She chuckled. 'You really are quite human, aren't you?' she said with satisfaction. 'I wasn't too sure when

I first met you yesterday,' she explained as he looked puzzled by her initial comment.

Nathan's expression was still perplexed. 'I think I would be wise not to pursue that remark by asking you why!'

'I think you would be too! So tell me, Nathan—' she sat forward, her pâté finished, resting her elbows on the table, her chin on her linked fingers '—if you don't want to discuss my mother, why did you invite me out to dinner?' She looked across at him with guileless eyes.

He was in the process of taking a prawn from its shell, but at her question his fingers fumbled over the task and he dropped the prawn back onto his plate, the shell still intact. 'Oh, to hell with this!' He impatiently dipped his fingers into the bowl of water that had been provided. 'I give up!' He sat back, his face grim. 'You're doing absolutely nothing for my digestion!'

He hadn't answered her question... And, Brianna guessed ruefully, he had no intention of doing so.

She leant forward to his plate and deftly removed the prawn from its shell. 'Here.' She held the fish out to him. 'I'm sure you didn't have lunch, either,' she encouraged as he continued to stare at her stony-faced.

Nathan slowly sat forward, his gaze locked with hers. 'Are you always this—?'

'Bossy?' she finished for him, putting the prawn back down on his plate as he made no effort to take it from her. She picked up another of the shellfish and starting to peel that one too. 'Probably.' She gave the same answer he had given her earlier.

'I was going to say straightforward,' he corrected, picking up the shelled prawn and eating it. 'But bossy fits just as well!' He looked at her with laughter in his eyes.

Oh, God, she hoped he didn't actually smile at her. If

he did, she would be lost. How awful that she should find herself so attracted to a man who was involved in her past, one she wasn't even sure she wanted to know about...!

'Are there any more at home like you?' she burst out, continuing to peel his prawns for him—something he seemed quite happy to let her do. 'I mean, do you have any brothers or sisters?' she corrected, as she realised she'd sounded as if she was being rude—again!

'I knew what you meant, Brianna,' he countered. 'And, no, there aren't any more at home like me. Like you, I'm an only child.'

She shook her head. 'I have a brother. His name's Gary. He's seventeen, and taking his "A" levels,' she deliberately corrected him.

'I'm sorry. I didn't mean— It must be nice to have a sibling,' he continued smoothly. 'I found it very lonely growing up as an only child. But, as my mother is fond of telling me—' his mouth twisted derisively '—going through childbirth once was quite enough for her. She had done her duty and given my father his son and heir!'

There was a wealth of feeling behind his words, and it was easy for Brianna to see what effect his mother had had on Nathan as he was growing up. Perhaps it was an indicator as to where Nathan had acquired his cool remoteness. He'd admitted he had grown up very lonely.

But she had also known what he meant earlier by the remark about them both being only children; she had been her natural mother's only child!

'My father tells me that most women feel the same way after the birth of their first child,' she told Nathan conversationally. 'But the feeling usually fades with time. My father is an obstetrician,' she supplied at his questioning look. 'It's ironic, really, that he should have specialised in that area of medicine once he had done his general training—considering the problems he and my mother had having a child of their own,' she added huskily.

Nathan gave her a searching look. 'Do you think so?'

'Don't you?' She had finished peeling all his prawns for him now, was washing her own fingers in the bowl of warm water.

'Not really.' Nathan shrugged. 'It's a bit like a scientist going into a particular area of research because a member of his family, or a close friend, died of that disease.'

'Or someone becoming a lawyer because a member of their family, or a close friend, was a crook,' Brianna returned mischievously. 'That way they would know how to beat the system!'

He frowned across at her. 'I've never thought of my profession in quite that way.'

Mr Pompous was back in evidence again! 'Haven't you?' she returned lightly. 'Was I being too irreverent for you?' she teased.

'It isn't that—'

'Oh, Nathan, life itself is far too serious,' she told him chidingly, knowing it most certainly *was* 'that'. 'If we didn't learn to laugh at it, we would get buried under all the problems thrown at us.'

'I didn't notice you laughing today in my father's office,' he said.

'No. Well.' She avoided his gaze. 'Maybe I didn't laugh then. But I will,' she added firmly. One day. When it was all firmly behind her.

'I'm sorry, Brianna.' Nathan reached out and clasped her hand again. 'That was very unfair of me. And I brought you out this evening with the intention of cheering you up,' he said self-disgustedly.

'So that's why you brought me out,' she accused teasingly. 'And I thought it was because you liked me!'

'I do! I mean— Brianna, you are like no one I've ever met before!' he responded, as he saw the laughter dancing in her eyes, removing his hand from hers to take a very necessary sip of the white wine he had ordered to accompany their meal.

'Or ever wish to meet again,' she guessed laughingly. 'What sort of women do you usually take out to dinner?' she asked interestedly, sitting back as their used plates were deftly removed by the waiter.

'Brianna—'

'I'm just curious, Nathan.' She interrupted his exasperation. She was curious as to why, at thirty-five, he was still a bachelor... At a guess, he was too picky, as her mother, Jean, used to put it.

He shook his head. 'It isn't usual to discuss the other women in one's life on a first date,' he told her coolly.

Mr Pompous again... 'Let's agree, I'm unusual—then you can answer the question!' She grinned as he still looked exasperated.

'I was engaged once,' he said tersely. 'I— It didn't work out. There haven't been too many women that I've taken out to dinner since then,' he added bleakly.

So he had been engaged to be married... Brianna couldn't help wondering what his fiancée had looked like, what she had been like, but one look at the challenge in his expression and she decided that for once discretion was advisable; at this rate Nathan wasn't going to finish his meal before leaving!

'How long ago was that?' she prompted.

'Five years,' he supplied defensively.

Her brows rose. 'Then I'm honoured by your invitation.' And she was. Although she had a feeling Nathan was regretting having made it!

He studied her face searchingly, as if sensing sarcasm in her remark. But he didn't find it in her expression—as it hadn't been in her remark. Brianna steadily met his probing gaze.

'You said "first date",' she recalled. 'Does that mean you're going to ask me out again?'

'Ask me that again at the end of the evening!' he choked incredulously, sitting back as their main course was served to them, obviously relieved at the diversion.

Brianna smiled unconcernedly. 'We may not be talking by the end of the evening!'

He held her eyes once they were alone again. 'I never sulk, Brianna,' he told her huskily. 'I say what I have to say, and that's the end of the subject.'

And she was sure that when he chose to say something he did it very pointedly!

But she was enjoying this evening with him. Despite the circumstances under which they had met, she liked him, she realized. She was very aware of him physically, her mind having wandered off several times this evening as she looked at him, seeing Nathan in her imagination in several situations of intimacy.

'So do I,' she told him lightly—although she had no intention of saying what she was thinking right now!

'I've noticed,' he said. 'Now, eat your food, before it gets cold!'

'Yes, sir!' she mocked—before proceeding to do so.

Nathan's choice of restaurant wasn't one known to her—but, considering their differences in lifestyle, that wasn't surprising! The food was delicious, and she ate it with great enjoyment, finally realising that Nathan was watching her now, rather than eating his own meal...

'What's wrong?' she asked warily. 'Do I have asparagus at the corner of my mouth or something?' she persisted self-consciously.

He smiled, shaking his head. 'I was just thinking you eat in the same way you seem to approach life—head-on!'

She shrugged. 'It's the way my parents brought me up.'

'I wasn't being disapproving, Brianna,' he assured her. 'It's very refreshing.'

And probably at complete odds with the way he had been brought up, she hazarded a guess. Parents, she realised, had to take a lot of responsibility for the way in which their children approached life. She, as Nathan had just pointed out, met it head-on, treating everything as a challenge, whereas Nathan was much more cautious.

Although she certainly hadn't met this situation over her real mother head-on...

She drew a ragged breath. 'Nathan, I know we agreed not to discuss Rebecca...'

'We did,' he acknowledged, he the one to look wary now.

She nodded. 'But there is one thing about her that I need to know...'

He put down his knife and fork, his own meal only half eaten. 'Brianna, it wouldn't be ethical for me to discuss any of this with you—'

'Because we're out together socially?'

He shook his head. 'Rebecca was my father's client. I only know some of the history because I know the family.'

She frowned. 'But what I want to know isn't anything to do with the legalities of the situation. In fact, it's a matter of public record. I just thought it might be—easier—' she sighed '—if you were the one to tell me.'

He swallowed hard, his expression sober. 'I'm not sure I want to be the one to tell you anything about your mother. I've only known you for two days, Brianna, and

I don't want to be the one to tell you something you're going to dislike me for afterwards!' he told her bluntly.

She met his gaze again steadily, deep blue matched against ice. 'I want to know how my mother died, Nathan,' she said huskily. 'She was only eighteen, for goodness' sake!' It was a question she had avoided asking earlier today, in his father's office, but now she wanted to know. Needed to know!

Nathan drew in a deeply controlling breath. 'I had a feeling it was going to be something like this,' he rasped, shaking his head. 'I can't tell you that—'

'But you can,' she interrupted vehemently. 'You know so much else about all of this, you must know how Rebecca died!' It had suddenly become very important that she knew too. It was probably the basis on which the rest of her decisions would be made. 'Please, Nathan.' She tightly clasped his hand. 'I have to know!'

'I wasn't going to say I wouldn't tell you, Brianna,' he said gently. 'Only that I can't tell you here, in the middle of a crowded restaurant.'

'I think it's the best place you could tell me,' she instantly disagreed. She didn't want to be anywhere where she could react too strongly; Rebecca was becoming a real person to her, in spite of herself, and knowing how she died could be traumatic.

Nathan looked at her searchingly. 'I would rather my father be the one to tell you.'

'And I don't want to hear it from your father,' she said with feeling.

Nathan drew in a ragged breath. 'Brianna, I really don't want to do this!' he protested forcefully.

'But you will,' she said with certainty.

He gave a shuddering sigh, obviously warring inwardly with himself. And then he gave an abrupt nod of his head. 'But I will,' he acknowledged wearily, turning his hand over so that it tightly clasped hers too now. 'Rebecca gave birth to you quite safely—put all thoughts of being in any way responsible for her death from your mind, Brianna,' he added gruffly as her face flooded with relief. 'Rebecca was young and healthy, your birth perfectly normal.'

Brianna shook her head dazedly. She had feared, when she dared to allow herself to think about it at all, that her own birth might have been the cause of Rebecca's death. Now she was more confused than ever...

She frowned. 'I don't understand...?'

Nathan's grip tightened on her hand. 'During the two months after your birth Rebecca set all her affairs in order—your adoption, the drawing up of her will. And then, two days after your adoption by the Gibsons, she...' He hesitated, obviously not at all happy about any of this.

'Tell me, Nathan,' Brianna said shakily, her eyes dark with emotion.

He sighed again. 'Two days after your adoption by the Gibsons,' he continued, 'Rebecca calmly walked directly into the path of an oncoming train.'

Brianna stared at him, at once horrorstruck and at the same time disbelieving.

Suicide...!

Rebecca had killed herself.

CHAPTER FOUR

'WE'RE getting out of here,' Nathan rasped savagely, signalling the waiter for their bill.

Brianna was barely aware of him paying it, of Nathan holding her arm as they left the restaurant, of getting into his waiting car outside.

Suicide. Rebecca had taken her own life.

Brianna didn't know what she had been expecting, but it certainly wasn't this! Rebecca had been, as Nathan described her, a young woman full of life, laughter and beauty. And yet she had killed herself. Why?

'Only Rebecca herself could tell you that,' Nathan answered her gently in the silent darkness of his car—the first indication Brianna had that she had actually spoken her anguish out loud. 'But I would hazard a guess at there being no reason for her to go on once she had given you up for adoption.'

'Then why did she?' Brianna cried out at the waste of such a young life. 'By all accounts she was a wealthy young woman. She could have kept me and herself quite comfortably. There was no reason for her to do what she did!'

Nathan shook his head. 'You're forgetting Giles,' he pointed out. 'He was furious when he found out Rebecca was pregnant, so much so that Rebecca ran away—from him, the only home she had ever known, the only family she had—to live in London until you were born. She was eighteen, Brianna,' he reminded her forcefully. 'Admittedly, she had the money left to her by her mother, but she was still only eighteen, barely capable of taking care of herself, let alone a newborn baby.'

'But—'

'Besides,' he continued heavily, 'she knew that Giles would eventually find her. And then he would either have forced her to give up her baby, or taken them both back to live with him. Which, in Rebecca's eyes, after the childhood she'd had, must surely have been a much worse option! She chose what she believed she would have been made to do anyway. And then she denied her father the one thing she knew would make him feel he had won; she died rather than go back to live in his home!'

It was barbaric. Inhuman. Brianna couldn't believe one man could exact such power over another human being. 'I hate him,' she said flatly. 'I hate him—and I've never met him.' She shuddered with revulsion. 'I'm sorry,' she added, her throat catching.

Nathan was watching her concernedly. 'I would say your reaction was perfectly understandable in the circumstances.'

'I'm not apologising for that. I appear to have hurt you.' She gingerly touched his hand, where she could clearly see the outline of two half-moon puncture marks in his skin, made by her nails when she had gripped his hand as he told her of how her mother had died. She had actually drawn blood! 'That must have hurt,' she whispered—and he hadn't so much as winced when she inflicted the wounds.

'You were hurting inside. It isn't important.'

Without really thinking what she was doing, Brianna bent down and kissed the two puncture marks. 'I really am sorry, Nathan,' she told him chokily.

'Brianna…!'

She looked up at him from beneath long lashes, her

eyes widening at the way his face had changed, at his eyes glowing palely blue. And he was suddenly closer, so very much closer. 'Nathan...?' She breathed shallowly, her heart pounding.

'Oh God...!' he groaned emotionally before his head bent and his mouth claimed hers, not savagely, or even hard, but with a tenderness that seemed to wrench the heart right out of her.

Brianna's arms moved up about his neck as she kissed him back. One of Nathan's hands moved to run lightly up and down the length of her spine, the other was entangled in the hair at her nape as he held her to him, deepening the kiss, passion flaring between them like a red-hot flame.

The Ice Man had melted, and in his place was a deeply sensual and tactile man, his caresses growing with the kiss, one hand cupping the underside of her breast now, even as his tongue moved erotically across the moist softness of her bottom lip.

Then suddenly he wrenched away, putting her firmly back on her side of the car before leaning back against the door behind him, his breathing ragged, his expression grim. 'That was a mistake,' he ground out.

Brianna knew that she was no longer pale; her cheeks were burning now, her lips slightly swollen from his kisses, her eyes glowing deeply blue, her body tingling from the caress of his hands. 'I agree, a car isn't exactly the right place to—'

'I wasn't referring to our location.' He straightened in his seat, turning the key to start the car. 'I'll take you home.'

Brianna stared at him. If he hadn't meant their location was wrong, then he must have meant that kissing her had been a mistake. In the circumstances, he was probably right. But it had only been a kiss, for goodness' sake; he didn't have to look quite so grim about it!

But Nathan did look grim. He wasn't just the Ice Man, but that remote stranger she had first met yesterday. As far as Brianna was concerned, that kiss apart, it was far too late for him to be like that. Nathan, it appeared, knew of her past as well as her present, and she knew so much more about him than had actually been said in words. Perhaps that was part of his problem too; Nathan didn't appear to be a man who let people close to him, either physically or emotionally.

The lights were on downstairs when they arrived back at Brianna's home, which meant her father probably hadn't gone to bed yet. Not that that mattered particularly; she had brought dates in before at the end of an evening. Although she somehow already knew what Nathan's answer to an invitation to come in for coffee would be…

'I'm in court tomorrow,' he predictably refused. 'I have some notes I have to go through when I get home.'

'Thank you for taking me out to dinner. I enjoyed it.'

His mouth visibly twisted in the light given off by the street-lamp outside on the pavement. 'I doubt that very much,' he returned dryly.

'But I did,' she protested; he was the one who hadn't eaten his meal.

Nathan reached out and briefly touched her cheek. 'Don't let all of this hurt or change you, Brianna,' he said huskily. 'Too much damage has already been done without that happening to you. Rebecca obviously chose to distance you from it all right from the beginning for that very reason.'

Brianna was puzzled. 'Then why involve me in it now?'

'Maybe she considered that at twenty-one you would be old enough to handle it.'

'And do you think I am?' Brianna returned sceptically.

'I hope so. When you're ready, I suggest you contact my father and arrange to hear Rebecca's will.'

And read her letter to you. He didn't add that, but it was there in his tone nonetheless...

His suggestion that she contact his father when she felt ready clearly stated that as far as he was concerned this was their first date and their last!

She couldn't help feeling disappointed about that. She liked Nathan, responded to him in a way she never had to any other man. But obviously he didn't feel the same way...

'I'll do that,' she answered briskly, opening the car door to get out onto the pavement. 'Take care, Nathan,' she added softly.

'Brianna!'

'Yes?' She turned back quickly at the sound of her name, wondering if he had changed his mind—not about coming in for coffee, but about the decision she was sure he had made not to see her again.

He drew in a harsh breath, his mouth a thin, straight line. 'You take care too,' he finally bit out.

She swallowed down her disappointment, summoning up a smile. 'I'll do that,' she assured him, continuing up the pathway to the house, aware as she unlocked the front door and let herself inside that he hadn't driven away yet; the Jaguar was still parked against the kerb.

She leant weakly back against the door once she had closed it behind her, finally hearing the soft purr of the Jaguar's engine as Nathan drove away, surprised when she found she was blinking back tears.

Why on earth was she crying? Because Nathan had

kissed her? No! She had enjoyed being kissed by him. Because Nathan hadn't asked her out again? They barely knew each other, so it couldn't be that, either. For Rebecca, then? For a young girl of eighteen, who hadn't been able to see a happy future for herself and her baby and who'd seen no future for herself at all without her baby? Yes... It was all so—

'Brianna?' Her father stepped enquiringly out of the sitting-room, frowning as he saw her standing so close to the door. 'I thought I heard you come in. Why are you standing out here?' He looked puzzled. 'It's not very— Brianna, are you crying?' He suddenly realised there were tears falling unchecked down her cheeks. 'Oh, love, don't cry!' he said as he held out his arms to her.

Brianna ran into them, a sob catching in her throat as she buried her face in the comfort of his shoulder. 'Rebecca—my mother—killed herself,' she choked. 'She was eighteen years old, and she killed herself!'

'I know, love.' Her father held her tightly. 'I know.'

She raised her head to look at him dazedly. 'You know...?'

He drew in a long breath, nodding slowly. 'Let's go into the sitting-room where it's warm.'

He kept his arm about the slenderness of her shoulders as he took her through into the warmth, where the book he had been reading lay open on the coffee table next to a half-finished glass of whisky.

'Dutch courage,' he explained as Brianna looked at the latter in surprise; her father rarely drank alcohol— being on call to his patients meant he couldn't risk the indulgence. 'I've been building myself up to this moment for weeks,' he confessed, as he firmly sat Brianna down in an armchair. 'Ever since that firm of solicitors wrote me for confirmation of your identity.' He shook his head, looking every one of his fifty-three years. 'Somehow your mother—Jean—'

'My mother,' she corrected quietly, still staring at her father. 'You knew Rebecca,' she guessed.

'Yes,' he confirmed shakily. 'Jean and I both knew her. And we thought—we always thought we would be together when the time came for us to talk to you about her.' He shook his head. 'These last few months have been—awful,' he said inadequately. 'And the last forty-eight hours have been a nightmare! Since Jean died two years ago, I had put all of this out of my head, didn't want you to know about—about that other family.' He grimaced. 'Maybe that was selfish of me.'

'No,' Brianna assured him. 'I think I can understand why you felt that way. I felt exactly the same way myself earlier today, when Peter Landris tried to talk to me about Rebecca.'

She still wasn't sure how her father and mother could ever have known Rebecca, was still stunned to learn that they had—she knew that it wasn't usual for adoptive parents to meet the natural mother. But, at the same time, she felt so sorry for her father that he'd had to carry all of this alone for the last few months. Her parents' marriage had always been a partnership; it had been difficult enough for him to function alone the last two years, without this added strain.

'You don't have to tell me any of this now, if you would rather not,' she comforted him.

He gave a sad smile. 'Dutch courage, remember. Besides, you have to know, Brianna. Half the truth is more destructive than none at all!'

She had to agree with him. It had been extremely difficult for her to listen to Peter Landris earlier today, so much so that in the end she had left before he had finished speaking. But now she was filled with a dozen questions she needed answers to. Some of which, she realised, her father might be able to answer...

She sat quietly as she waited for him to begin talking, letting him do it in his own time. Despite his Dutch courage, she knew it couldn't be easy for him. Besides, there was no hurry; she had already waited twenty-one years and she could certainly wait a while longer!

Her father didn't sit down, but paced about restlessly in front of the fire. 'I was working in a hospital twenty-one years ago,' he began. 'And your mother worked in the X-ray department. We had been married six years by that time, for three of which we had been trying to have a baby. We had tests, and it was discovered that I have a low sperm count, that the possibility of us having a child of our own was pretty remote. We explored the avenue of adoption and were found to be suitable candidates; all we had to do was wait until a baby became available. Then a young girl came into the hospital for her routine check-up when she was eighteen weeks pregnant—'

'Rebecca,' Brianna realised.

'Rebecca,' he confirmed heavily. 'It was all done legally, Brianna. Rebecca wasn't my patient. But the one thing she was adamant about was that she was going to put her baby up for adoption, that she wanted to give her child the best chance of happiness that she could.'

'She did,' Brianna assured him emotionally, knowing Rebecca couldn't have picked two finer people to become her baby's parents than the Gibsons.

And Rebecca had chosen them carefully; Brianna knew that without a doubt. There had been no abandoning of her baby, no ridding herself of her unwanted child; Rebecca had known exactly who she was giving her daughter to...

'Thank you,' her father accepted gruffly. 'We spent

months getting to know Rebecca. Jean was with her at your birth. And she came to live with us for two weeks after you were born. Then she went off on her own with you for several weeks before the time came for her to hand you over to us. Jean was distraught at letting you go, even for that short time, but we both knew we owed at least that much to Rebecca. Six weeks after she left us, when the adoption was all legalised, she came back, calmly handed you over to us—and we never saw her again.' He paused. 'Rebecca died two days later.'

Brianna knew exactly how she had died! Rebecca had waited until she had safely settled her daughter with her adoptive parents, and then she had taken her own life. Because, without her baby, she'd had nothing left to live for...

'Did she ever tell you who her baby's father was?' Brianna persisted intently.

'She refused to name him, because he was married to someone else.' Brianna's father shook his head. 'She said it would help no one and hurt too many people.'

'But she was hurting,' Brianna protested. 'She had nothing left to live for!'

'We tried, Brianna,' her father answered raggedly. 'Jean and I talked to her for hours at a time. Even though we dearly wanted you as our own, we felt that with a little emotional support Rebecca might have been able to keep you herself. But she said too many people had been hurt already, that if she kept you it would only get worse. She refused to name your father, Brianna, and put down ''Unknown'' in that column on your original birth certificate. But she did choose your name herself, asked if we would mind that. Mind!' There were tears glistening in his eyes. 'As if we cared what your name was! You were adorable, and you were going to be our child, it was the least we could do to let Rebecca name you!'

Brianna... As Nathan had remarked earlier today, it was an unusual name...

'There's something else, Brianna.' Her father paused again. 'Something I'm not sure Peter Landris or his son has told you yet. I think not, from what you've told me.'

Something else? What else could there possibly be to tell?

'When Rebecca came to the hospital she was registered as Rebecca Jones. But when the adoption went through, we discovered that wasn't her name at all.' He swallowed hard. 'Her surname was Mallory. And her mother's maiden name, before she married Giles Mallory, had been Harrington.'

Brianna looked at him blankly. He said it as if it should mean something to her, and yet it didn't. Why should it?

Harrington... Nathan had said her grandmother had been the daughter of a rich family, that Joanne had come to her marriage with money. But—Harrington!

She looked sharply across at her father, disbelief reflected in her eyes. It couldn't be. He didn't mean *that* Harrington!

'Harrington Press,' her father supplied gently.

He did mean that Harrington!

'Apparently Joanne Harrington had an older brother who inherited the publishing empire,' her father continued flatly. 'But Joanne herself was left a considerable shareholding in it, shares she left, on her death, to her daughter Rebecca, along with a great amount of money.'

Brianna swallowed hard, moistening dry lips. 'Nathan mentioned Rebecca's will. You don't think...? No.' She shook her head in denial, giving an inner shudder. She didn't want any part of that other life!

Her father came down on his haunches beside her, firmly grasping her restless hands. 'Rebecca told us about her will. Of course we never expected that she would— Her death only days afterwards, came as a shock to us,' he said regretfully. 'I know that the shares in Harrington press were given back to her uncle on her death, and that she willed the bulk of the money to her father, but—she insisted on leaving you a legacy, Brianna. It was left in trust for you. But I have no idea how much it was.'

'She left me a letter.' Brianna's eyes were huge and haunted in her suddenly pale face as she remembered what Nathan had said to her earlier today—'You stand to be a very wealthy woman at the end of this conversation...' So, Rebecca had left not just a letter! 'This is incredible, Dad.' She turned her head away in denial of what she was hearing. 'And you've always known about this?'

'We knew that when you were twenty-one you were to inherit something from your mother,' he admitted. 'We never knew what—and we didn't want to know. We just wanted to be a normal family, to bring you up as our daughter, and, when the time came, Jean and I had intended to tell you about all of this together. I should have done it months ago, but somehow I just couldn't do it without Jean. I know it was wrong of me, but I—I just wanted to keep you as our daughter for as long as possible!'

'Oh, Daddy!' She used her childhood name for him, turning back and launching herself into his arms. 'I'll always be your daughter, yours and Mum's,' she assured him emotionally. 'Can't you see that this was what Rebecca wanted for me?' She looked up at him with tear-wet cheeks. 'She wanted me to be your daughter, brought up in a house full of love and laughter. I *am* your daughter, yours and Mum's!'

But she also knew she had to read Rebecca's letter now, that she owed her that much; Rebecca had sacrificed too much for Brianna to deny her now...

'Have I ruined your lunch-break for a second time?' Brianna smiled at the frowning man sitting across the desk from her.

'It isn't that,' Peter Landris dismissed. 'I rarely eat lunch, anyway.'

She stilled. 'Is the documentation I just showed you not in order?'

'Perfectly in order.' It had taken him all of two minutes to peruse the birth certificate and adoption papers Brianna had brought with her today.

'Then why do you still seem so—pensive?' Brianna prompted warily.

'I find your request that Nathan be here too a little—unorthodox.'

Her eyes widened. 'This whole situation is unorthodox, Mr Landris,' she pointed out. 'For the last twenty-one years you have kept to yourself the knowledge of Rebecca's last will and testament.' Now she wanted to hear it. But she wanted Nathan to be there. Needed him there.

'That's what lawyers do, Miss Gibson,' he told her tersely, obviously not at all happy with her rebuke. 'And your remark wasn't completely accurate. It's only in relation to you that Rebecca's will has been outstanding. And that is for obvious reasons. You only recently attained the age of twenty-one, and so I didn't—'

'Sorry I'm late.' Nathan burst unannounced into the room, dressed, as he had told Brianna the night before, for court in a dark jacket and dark striped trousers.

'Brianna,' he greeted gravely, his eyes once again hidden behind the barrier of his glasses.

She was starting to dislike those glasses intensely. She had a feeling Nathan didn't wear them just for reading at all, that he was well aware of the defence they put between him and the rest of the world. At the moment between him and her.

'Nathan,' she returned brightly. 'In case I didn't thank you for dinner last night, it was delicious,' she tacked on mischievously; let him put a barrier up against that!

He shot a quick glance at his father, his mouth tight as he turned back to her. 'You did thank me,' he grated.

'Dinner?' his father repeated predictably, sharply. 'The two of you had dinner together last night?'

'I believe that's what Brianna just said, yes,' Nathan snapped, challenge in his expression as he met his father's censorious gaze.

'I see,' his father bit out—obviously not seeing at all. 'Well, as you know, Brianna has requested that you be here for this meeting, so I suppose we had better get on with it.'

Not a happy man, Brianna decided. She hadn't for a moment thought he would be when she had telephoned first thing that morning and asked to speak to him some time that day. She'd asked for Nathan to be there too. She wanted Nathan present. Despite the way in which they had parted last night, she needed him to be here.

'I spoke to my father last night,' she told both men. 'I know now that my maternal grandmother was Joanne Harrington before she married. I'm not interested in that side of Rebecca's will,' she added firmly as Peter Landris started to speak. 'I only want to read the letter Rebecca left for me.' Her hands shook slightly as she clasped them together in her lap.

She had lain awake thinking about this most of last

night, hadn't really slept much, but she had decided that the sooner she read Rebecca's letter to her then the sooner she would know what she was going to do next. If anything.

'The money that was left to you has been held in trust—'

'I'm not interested in the money, only the letter!' Brianna's eyes flashed as she glared at Peter Landris.

'It's a considerable sum—'

'I don't care how much it is,' she cut in firmly. 'I have everything I could possibly want; I don't need that money.'

'But—'

'Father, I think you should leave that side of this alone for the moment,' Nathan spoke up. He had obviously seen the light of battle in Brianna's eyes, and, unlike his father, had taken heed of it. 'There will be time at a later date to discuss that with Brianna, maybe set up a trust fund for her own children if she still decides she doesn't want it—don't be so damned hasty, Brianna!' he rasped as she began to protest again. 'No matter what other mistakes she may have made, Rebecca did all that she could for her child—you! Don't throw that back in her face.'

'Nathan!' his father reproved sternly, deeply displeased by his son's lack of professionalism.

Nathan looked unperturbed by the rebuke, still looking at Brianna. 'Be stubborn if you want, Brianna,' he told her bluntly. 'But don't be stupid.'

'Nathan, I really must protest—'

'It's all right, Mr Landris,' Brianna assured the older man softly, a smile curving her lips as she returned Nathan's gaze. 'Nathan and I understand each other.' That was why she wanted him here today. Nathan might be trying to put a distance between them, for reasons she didn't fully understand, but he couldn't deny the rapport that existed between them. Even if he did want to deny the passion they had shared last night... 'I'll try not to be stupid, Nathan,' she told him mock-contritely.

He gave her a narrow-eyed look before giving an abrupt nod of his head. 'I'm glad to hear it.'

She held back her smile with effort. He really could be incredibly pompous—and yet she liked him. Perhaps more than was actually wise, in these strange circumstances. And obviously to his father's dismay... But she couldn't help that.

She turned back to his father. 'The letter, Mr Landris,' she prompted huskily.

He had a file open on his desk, and a letter lay at the top of it. 'I have no idea what is written here.' He picked the envelope up in hands, Brianna noticed abstractedly, that were very much like his son's: long and elegant. 'And I think you might prefer to read it in private, so—'

'No!' she denied sharply, too sharply. 'No,' she repeated less forcefully. 'I would prefer that you both remain.'

Peter Landris raised surprised brows. At the same time he nodded acquiescence, passing the letter across the desk to her.

Brianna just held it for several seconds, not even looking at it, just acknowledging it was the one thing she had ever received—or ever would receive—from her real mother. She knew she was so much luckier than most adopted children, who, in the worst scenario, discovered a mother who was alarmed by their reappearance. She knew from her adoptive father that had never been the case with Rebecca.

Only one word adorned the front of the envelope. Her name. Brianna. The name her mother had given her before she died.

Her hands trembled as she opened the envelope, shaking quite noticeably as she took out the single sheet of notepaper. And, for all that Nathan and his father were in the room with her, at her own request, she might as well have been alone as she read the only words her mother ever said to her.

'My darling daughter,' the letter began, and Brianna felt tears in her eyes, her throat moving convulsively as she read the rest of the letter.

I hope you will allow me to call you that, because you were my own dearly beloved child from the moment I knew I had conceived you. I loved you then, as I love you now. I wish—oh, how I wish I could have kept you, watched you grow into the beautiful woman I am sure you have become. But it isn't to be, too much pain has been caused already. Instead I have given you the life you deserve. Jean and Graham will be good parents to you, I am sure, and will bring you up with the same wonderful values they have themselves. Best of all, I know they will love you as their own.

I haven't lived wisely, Brianna. But, until you came, I only hurt myself with my mistakes. Please believe you were conceived with love, on my side, if not your father's. You have to know the worst of it, and I hope you will be able to forgive me. Your father was married to someone else, but I, in my naïveté, believed he would come to love me. Once I knew we were to have a child, I thought he would come to me, that we would be the family I had always wanted. I was wrong. So terribly wrong. In the circumstances, I had no choice but to leave my home, to hide myself away until you were born.

I have done that now. I felt you grow inside me,

knew the movements of you, gave birth to you, nursed you for the first two months of your life. But now it's time for me to let you go, into the loving care of Jean and Graham. It's my last act of love for you, my darling daughter. My one and only gift to you. Always know that I loved you. I hope that you will always be happy.

Your loving mother,

Rebecca.

Brianna stared at the letter, slowly reading it again. There was so much Rebecca had missed out. Her own awful childhood. The fact that she'd had to leave home because her own father was such a despot. The identity of Brianna's own father!

None of those things was written there. But the slight smudges on the letter were easily identifiable as tears having fallen on the notepaper as it was being written. Brianna could feel her own tears falling hotly down her cheeks...

The one thing she was absolutely and positively sure about was that Rebecca had loved her deeply. Enough to find life wasn't worth living once she had seen her baby settled. Brianna also knew that it needn't have been that way, that it could all have been so different.

She folded the letter neatly back into four before placing it in its envelope, her expression hard when she finally looked up at the two Landris men, the father seeming alarmed, the son watchfully cautious.

Why?

But Brianna knew the answer to that question even as she asked it. Neither of these men were comfortable with raw emotion. And she did feel raw, so much so that she wanted to hit out and hurt someone. But not physically. She wanted to hurt someone as Rebecca had been hurt.

'Brianna?' Nathan questioned.

'Nathan,' she returned. She hadn't needed him here after all, was perfectly in control again now.

'Was the letter—of any help to you?' Peter Landris asked lightly.

Help? No, she doubted it had been that. But it had settled something in her mind, something of which she had been unsure but of which she was now absolutely certain.

'Not really,' she replied, opening her handbag and putting the letter safely away inside. She would read it again later, when she was alone. 'Once again, I thank you for your time, gentlemen.' She stood up. 'I won't be bothering either of you again.'

'Brianna!' Nathan's exasperated rebuke stopped her at the door. 'I— You look—different.' He frowned. 'Rebecca's letter...'

'A letter from a mother leaving her daughter,' she told him coolly. 'Very sad. Very, very sad, as it happens. And deeply personal to me,' she added with finality.

'You don't think we, as Rebecca's lawyers, should see it?' Peter Landris was on his feet now.

'I don't think what I intend to do next concerns Rebecca's lawyers at all,' Brianna returned calmly.

She would read the letter again when she was alone. She would perhaps weep some more. But, as far as she was concerned, the Landris family's involvement in this was over.

'What you intend to do next?' Nathan picked up on the part of her statement he felt was important.

He was right, of course. But then, he was always right...

She reached out for the door handle, glancing back at Nathan, although she didn't really see him, her thoughts all flooding inwards. 'It's quite simple, Nathan,' she told him flatly. 'I intend to find out who my father is.'

'What?' Peter Landris gasped incredulously.

'Brianna, you can't be serious!' Nathan rasped harshly.

'This is hardly a time when I would be making jokes, Nathan,' she scorned. 'And especially about such a subject.'

'But—but why?' Peter Landris cried. 'It can serve no purpose now. Rebecca is dead—'

'Exactly,' she said. 'And my father, whoever he is, is the one responsible for her death. I intend finding him and acquainting him with that fact!' She turned and walked out of the office without a second glance, filled with a burning anger she had never known before.

She would find the man who had fathered her. He might think he was safe and snug in his marriage—secure!—but she would find him!

CHAPTER FIVE

'I THINK you should give yourself some time,' Nathan told her, once more behind the wheel of his car as he drove her back to the hospital—this time minus his glasses! He had followed her from his father's office, insisted, despite Brianna's protestations of it not being necessary, that he would drive her. 'To give you time to calm down. To take all of this in—'

'I don't need time to calm down, Nathan,' Brianna told him flatly. 'I'm not *un*calm. It seems perfectly logical to me that, having found my natural mother, I'm now curious about my natural father.'

Nathan gave her a grim glance. 'But this isn't being done out of curiosity, is it?' he muttered tensely.

Brianna sat unmoving at his side. Revenge. He was talking about revenge. And he was completely wrong. She wasn't a vengeful type of person.

Then why did she want to do this? She shied away from answering that question, even for herself. Perhaps Nathan was right. Perhaps she did need time to stop and consider all of this. It was just that the letter was so—so—

'Oh God, Brianna, are you crying again?' Nathan groaned, before he turned the car out of the flow of the traffic and drove into the hospital grounds, stopping at the front entrance. 'I can't stand it when you cry,' he said as he pulled her into the warm comfort of his arms.

Brianna wasn't even sure why she was crying. Maybe because, in spite of the letter, and the emotion and love that had been there for her, she still didn't know

Rebecca. She could feel pity for that young eighteen-year-old girl, could wish she had known her, that she had been able to love her. But the truth of the matter was that Rebecca hadn't been her mother; Jean Gibson had, and always would be...

'She was so alone, Nathan,' she choked against his shoulder. 'So very alone.'

'All of her life,' Nathan confirmed.

Brianna drew in a controlling breath, moving away from him, the tears drying on her cheeks. 'I'm going to see her father,' she told him determinedly.

'He won't want to see you,' Nathan told her knowingly. 'Giles has become even more reclusive over the years. He's rarely seen. And he sees no one.'

'He'll see me,' she said firmly.

Nathan shrugged. 'Not without a fight.'

She gave a wry smile. 'Haven't you noticed? I can be pretty determined when I decide to do something.' As evidenced by the fact that she had managed to see the two 'unavailable' Landris men twice in two days!

'Yes, I've noticed,' Nathan acknowledged dryly. 'But Giles is something else,' he added. 'You've already been hurt by what you already know; I wouldn't like to see you hurt any more than you need to be.'

'I'm his grandchild,' Brianna pointed out stubbornly.

'A grandchild he didn't want twenty-one years ago—'

'And still doesn't want,' she finished knowingly. 'Well, it appears to me that Giles has had things too much his own way for far too long! It's time all that changed.'

'He's too old to change, Brianna.' Nathan shook his head. 'He's seventy years old, as cantankerous as they come; I can assure you there won't be any last-minute reconciliations because of emotional contrition on his part! He didn't even attend Rebecca's funeral,' he informed her.

Brianna drew in a sharp breath. How could the man not have even gone to his own child's funeral? Especially when she was sure he was partially responsible for her death. But she didn't really know why she was surprised at this revelation; it fitted in with everything else she had heard about the man so far!

'I still intend going to see him,' she told Nathan doggedly.

He studied her in silence for several seconds, the determination in her eyes, the stubborn set to her mouth. Finally, he assented. 'I can see that you do.' He sighed. 'In that case, I'll take you there. This weekend, if that's convenient for you?'

Her eyes widened. 'Nathan, you've been very kind during all of this, but I really can't impose on you to that extent.' She shook her head.

'It's no trouble, Brianna,' he assured her. 'I intend going to Claremont this weekend, anyway. It's no problem if you come with me.'

'Claremont?' She frowned. 'Is that the name of the village where my grandfather lives?' And, if it was, why was Nathan going there? He had said her grandfather saw no one, so why would Nathan be going to see him this weekend? She didn't understand any of this...

'Claremont is the name of my parents' house,' Nathan explained patiently. 'Giles lives in the house next door. The Harringtons came from the north of England, and the house in Berkshire was a family holiday home, because it's so conveniently close to London. It was given to Giles and Joanne as their house when they married,' he continued as Brianna still looked confused. 'As Claremont was given to *my* father, the eldest son, when he married my mother. That's how the two families know each other so well.'

She was having trouble taking all of this in. The Landrises and the Mallorys had lived next door to each other for years—when Peter Landris and Joanne Harrington had been young, before either of them married other people, before either Nathan or Rebecca were born...

Peter Landris had seemed to know so much about the Mallory family, and Brianna had assumed—erroneously, it now turned out!—that this knowledge came from his legal dealings with them. It hadn't even occurred to her that the two families could be next-door neighbours...! And neither Nathan or his father had explained, until this moment, their connection. It put everything in a slightly different light, and she looked warily at Nathan now.

'Stop looking at me like that,' he rasped harshly. 'My father and uncle were always friendly with the Harringtons; apparently Joanne used to go around with the two of them when she stayed next-door for holidays. It worked out very well when she and my father stayed neighbours after their marriages.'

'I'm sure it did,' Brianna replied. 'But if you all knew the unhappiness that existed in the Mallory household, if your father and my grandmother were such good friends, why didn't someone in the Landris family try to do something to stop it?' she said accusingly, at last understanding some of Peter Landris's vehemence where Joanne and Rebecca's deaths were concerned. 'Giles was a despot, unkind to his wife, indifferent to his daughter—'

'Unkindness and indifference are not legal reasons for interfering in a marriage—'

'Legal reasons!' she scorned heatedly, eyes deeply blue. 'How about humanitarian ones? How about—?'

'Brianna,' Nathan cut in soothingly. 'I understand your distress—'

'Do you?' she returned scornfully. 'I doubt that very much!'

'Listen to me!' Nathan grasped her arm before she could thrust open the car door and get out onto the driveway. 'It was for Joanne to make the decisions you're talking about. Anyone else's interference would only have made things worse for Joanne and Rebecca—'

'It doesn't sound to me as if Joanne was capable of making those sort of decisions.'

'You're only seeing what you want to see, Brianna.' Nathan's hands tightened on her arms. 'Of course we all tried to help them, in the ways that were available to us. But, believe it or not, Joanne loved her husband. And Rebecca didn't spend all her school holidays alone in the house with the housekeeper; during the day she spent her time at our home. The two of us went fishing together. Played cricket—'

'Climbed trees?' Brianna put in, some of her anger abating as she imagined Nathan and her mother doing those things together. Now she just had more to feel sad about, and come to terms with.

'Rebecca was a tomboy until she got to about fifteen,' Nathan recalled. 'Until she discovered the opposite sex. And I don't mean me,' he muttered as Brianna raised her brows. 'At eleven, I was too damned young for her to even realise I was male!'

'Despite all that fishing and playing cricket?' Brianna teased.

'Brianna—'

'I was only teasing, Nathan.' She sobered, shaking her head. 'Not a very good attempt, I'll grant you, but— I'll think about your invitation for the weekend. Thank you

for asking me. At the moment I just need a little time
to sit and reflect on what I've learnt today.'

He released her. 'I can understand that. I think it's a
good idea that you do. But there will probably be quite
a crowd at my parents' house this weekend—there usually is—so you don't have to feel in the least awkward
about staying there. My uncle Roger and aunt Clarissa
will be there. And probably my aunt Susan too, my uncle
James's widow. You don't have to worry,' he continued,
seeing Brianna's horrified expression, 'it's a large
house!'

Of course it was a large house; the Landris family
were hardly likely to live in a three-bedroom detached
house like the one she shared with her father and
brother…!

'And none of them need know who you are and why
you're there, if you would rather they didn't,' Nathan
finished lightly.

'Your father knows exactly who I am.'

Nathan's mouth twisted wryly. 'I'm sure he will be
quite happy to keep your identity between the three of
us.'

Of course he would; Peter Landris had made it more
than obvious already that he found all of this very disturbing; he was hardly likely to want to distress the rest
of his family with the awkwardness of this situation!

She nodded. 'I'll ring you and let you know what I
decide to do. Thanks for the lift back to work,' she told
him as she finally got out of the car turning to hurry up
the hospital steps, once again late back from lunch.

'New boyfriend, Brianna?'

She turned to smile at the man who fell into step beside her—Jim, the junior doctor she had dated several
months ago. 'Just a friend,' she dismissed lightly—it was

too complicated to even begin to explain all of this to a
third party!

Jim glanced admiringly at the green Jaguar as Nathan
drove away. 'Nice car,' he observed.

Yes, it was a nice car. The man who drove it she still
wasn't sure of. She was attracted to Nathan, she couldn't
deny that, but there were still so many things about him,
and this situation, that she just didn't know...

'As I explained to you on the telephone when you decided to accept my invitation, my parents' home is only
in Berkshire.' Nathan chatted amiably as he drove. 'My
father drives from there into the city every day.'

'And, presumably, out again every evening,' Brianna
remarked.

He shot her an impatient glance. 'Yes,' he confirmed
tightly.

She hadn't meant to sound sarcastic, although she
could tell by Nathan's response that she must have
sounded exactly that. But she couldn't help it, she felt
very tense.

She *had* decided to accept Nathan's invitation to stay
the weekend at his parents' home; after careful thought
she had decided he was probably right, that this was the
best way to approach the situation.

Her father had been most unhappy at the thought of
her going to see her maternal grandfather. But once she
had shown him Rebecca's letter, and they had cried
about it together, he had accepted that this weekend was
something she felt she had to go through. She had left
home this afternoon with his best wishes.

Which was why she was once again sitting beside
Nathan in his Jaguar, on a warm Saturday afternoon in
late April, the bright colours of the wild spring flowers

that adorned the roadside doing nothing to alleviate her nervousness.

'How do your parents feel about your bringing me with you for the weekend?' She turned to Nathan—a more relaxed Nathan today, in faded denims and a pale blue open-necked shirt, his jacket taken off for the drive and laid on the back seat.

Nathan's mouth tightened slightly. 'Absolutely fine.'

Brianna looked at him searchingly. 'You don't sound very sure...?'

'Of course I'm sure,' he replied tersely. 'They were absolutely delighted that I was bringing a young lady down with me for the weekend.'

A young lady... 'You didn't tell either of them it was me,' she guessed knowingly.

His hands tightened on the steering wheel. 'It's my home too, Brianna,' he snapped. 'I'm at liberty to invite who I like there.'

'But—'

'My father may have put two and two together and come up with the appropriate answer,' he said quickly, as if impatient with the subject, 'but my mother has probably forgotten the existence of Rebecca's daughter, so I could hardly tell her that's who you are,' he defended at her censorious look.

'Your father won't have discussed all of this with her?' Brianna pressed.

'Did your father discuss his patients with your mother?' Nathan returned sharply.

'*Touché*, Nathan,' she acknowledged dryly. 'Only in the abstract,' she conceded. 'Allowing for doctor-patient confidentiality.'

'Lawyers have the same code of confidentiality,' he explained tersely. 'And if my father had talked to my mother about any of this—even in the abstract!—she would have realised who he was talking about. I was thinking of you, Brianna,' he snapped as she still frowned. 'I've assured you that no one—apart from my father, for obvious reasons—need even know who you are, let alone why you're there. You've had enough trauma for one week,' he observed accurately, 'without the speculation of my family to deal with. As I predicted the other day, they're all going to be there this weekend.'

'I wasn't frowning because of that.' She reached out and lightly touched his hand as it rested on the steering-wheel. 'I was thinking of the speculation you've now left yourself open to. Don't you see, Nathan?' she explained, 'if you haven't told them who I am, and why I'm there, then they are all going to assume I'm—well—that I'm the current woman in your life!'

His eyes narrowed. 'They can think what they damn well like!'

She knew he was arrogant enough to rise above that speculation, but even so... 'How many women have you taken home to meet your family in the last five years?' she prompted gently.

'None.'

That was what she had gathered from the remarks he had made the other evening concerning the ending of his engagement and the years since. He might dismiss his family's interest in his romantic life, but, if his mother was anything like her own had been, then of course she was going to speculate about his bringing a woman home for the weekend. Nathan was being very naïve if he thought otherwise. But if he was happy with that scenario, who was she to quibble about it...?

The Landris house, as Nathan had told her the other day, was big. In fact it wasn't just big, it was huge!

Claremont stood at the end of a half-mile, tree-lined driveway, a mellow-stoned manor house, surrounded by extensive and well-tended gardens, with several cars already parked on the driveway directly in front of it.

'Damn,' Nathan muttered as he spotted a red open-topped sportscar parked between a Mercedes and a BMW. 'My cousin Samantha is here,' he explained at Brianna's questioning look. 'Uncle James's and Aunt Susan's daughter' he supplied tersely, as he got out of the car to open Brianna's door for her. 'She must have driven Aunt Susan down,' he sighed as he took Brianna's overnight bag from the boot of the car. 'Now there will be some speculation, and it won't be silent either. Sam loves to tease me.' He grimaced with feeling, turning to lead the way over to the front door.

Brianna hadn't said a word since Nathan turned the car into the long driveway. Because she couldn't! She had come to realise, from their law practice, from the car Nathan drove, from the restaurants he obviously liked to frequent, that the Landris family were wealthy, but this house was something else! It stood completely on its own, in its own grounds, was probably run by an army of servants and gardeners—and it made her accusations the other day about the Landrises not being concerned about their neighbours' unhappiness seem slightly absurd; there wasn't another house in sight of this one, so goodness knew what was meant in this area by next-door neighbours!

As if guessing some of her thoughts, Nathan turned before opening the huge oak front door. 'Giles lives half a mile away in that direction.' He pointed off to the left. 'I thought we might take a walk over there tomorrow morning,' he suggested.

Nathan was going to come with her, she realised with a sense of relief. If the Mallory home was anywhere near as imposing as this one, then she would be glad of his support. It was going to take every ounce of courage she had to go there at all, let alone unaccompanied.

'Thank you.' She accepted the plan gratefully.

He looked down at her searchingly, putting down her bag to take a step closer to her. 'It's only a house, Brianna,' he told her. 'And the people inside it are just like any other family; their lives are full of insecurities, secrets, disappointments. And it's true what they say, you know.' His arms moved about her comfortingly as he still sensed her uncertainty. 'Money is fine, but it can't buy you happiness.'

Brianna had been resting her head on his chest, but now she looked up at him, smiling. 'But it can make life a lot easier while you're feeling unhappy!' she returned mischievously.

He smiled back down at her, that heart-stopping smile that fascinated Brianna every time he gave it. 'Probably,' he conceded dryly.

'Definitely!' She warmly returned his smile.

'My God, Brianna…!' He shook his head. 'What am I going to do with you?' he asked a little desperately—before his mouth came down demandingly on hers, answering his own question most satisfactorily!

She had, she realised, been waiting for this moment since the last time Nathan had kissed her, instantly responding, instinctively, as if this was exactly where she belonged. At this moment, that was exactly how it felt, her body melting against his, her arms up about his neck as she returned the passionate intensity of his kiss. It was as if they—

'My goodness, Nathan,' drawled an amused feminine voice. 'And on your own doorstep too!'

Brianna's initial reaction was to pull away guiltily, embarrassed at being caught in such an intimate situation. But Nathan wouldn't allow her to pull away, slowly ending the kiss, his arm still protectively about her waist, as they turned to confront their interloper.

A young woman stood in the now open doorway, probably aged in her mid-twenties, a blaze of red hair framing a gaminely beautiful face—a face dominated by pale blue eyes. Landris eyes, Brianna noted.

'You must be Samantha.' Brianna held out her hand in polite greeting, having guessed the identity of the newcomer by a simple process of elimination; she was young enough to be Samantha, and she did like to tease Nathan; those blue eyes were dancing now!

'Call me Sam,' she invited cheerfully, shaking Brianna's hand warmly. 'And you have to be Nathan's "young lady". That's the way my mother described the guest Nathan was bringing with him,' she added with a confiding grin. 'Once I heard that, I just had to come and see for myself! Hello, cuz.' She reached up and gave Nathan a hug and a kiss.

'Sam,' he returned briskly.

'We are all sitting out on the terrace, as it's such a lovely day. We heard your car in the driveway,' she chattered as she turned and walked back into the house, expecting them to follow her—which they did. 'I hope you've warned the poor girl about meeting the family *en masse* like this, Nathan,' she mocked, that gamine face full of mischief as she gave Nathan another teasing smile. 'They've scared off more than one of my boyfriends in the past!'

'I wouldn't be absolutely sure that was the family!' he returned like lightning.

'Pig!' Sam turned briefly and punched him lightly on the arm.

The two of them sounded like Brianna and her brother, Gary—a hint of normality in the midst of a situation that was fast becoming unreal to her as a manservant appeared, as if by magic, to relieve them of their jackets and take Brianna's overnight bag to be delivered to 'Miss Gibson's room'.

Sam raised her eyebrows as Nathan directed all this, linking her arm companionably through Brianna's. 'What else do they call you, besides Miss Gibson?' She gave a rueful shake of her head at Nathan's formality. 'Mother and I like to live comfortably, but nowhere near as grandly as this!' She almost seemed to be apologising for that very grandness.

And 'grand' did describe it very well. Brianna wondered how anyone could ever become accustomed to such a lifestyle. She decided that you had to be born to it to be at all comfortable with it. Not that she wanted to be part of it. She was only here for the weekend, after all, so she might as well enjoy the luxury of not having to cook meals, or do the washing-up afterwards, or do the housework, her usual weekend chore after a busy week at work.

'Brianna,' she supplied a little breathlessly, deciding that Sam was a little like a human dynamo as she swept her along at her side through the beautifully furnished house, presumably in the direction of the terrace, where the rest of this slightly forbidding-sounding family awaited their arrival—probably as curiously as Sam!

'What a great name,' Sam returned instantly. 'I hate the name Samantha.' She wrinkled her nose with feeling. 'I can't think what Mummy and Daddy were thinking of at the time. They could have give me an interesting name, like yours, and—'

'Hands off, Sam.' Nathan had finally caught up with them, gently but firmly releasing Brianna from his cousin's grasp. 'Brianna came here to spend the weekend with me, not listen to your incessant chatter!'

'Incessant chat—!' Sam broke off her indignant explosion as Nathan grinned at her, glaring at him with eyes so similar to his they might have been brother and sister—their behaviour certainly pointed to that kind of relationship. Although Sam had to get her red hair from her mother's side of the family, Brianna decided, because the members of the Landris family she had met so far were both very dark.

'I see you still have the temper to go with this.' Nathan lightly pulled one of those fiery red curls.

Sam gave a rueful smile. 'He's always been a terrible tease!' she confided to Brianna.

A tease? Nathan? Brianna looked at him questioningly. Now he didn't seem like the pompous Ice Man she had met that first day in his office, but a tease…? She wasn't sure he was that uncomplicated, either. In fact, she was sure he wasn't!

'Don't tell Brianna all my bad points just yet,' he jokingly chided his cousin.

'No doubt she'll discover them for herself soon enough,' Sam returned with a conspiratorial wink at Brianna. 'I really hope you're prepared for the lions' den,' she went on, as they reached a door that had to lead out onto the terrace. 'They're my family—and I still find them daunting!' But the arrogant way in which she pushed the door open to rejoin her family totally belied that claim!

Brianna hung back at Nathan's side, nowhere near as confident as the other woman. These people might not know who she actually was, but even so they believed her to be a close friend of Nathan's, which was almost as bad! They couldn't help but look at her critically, and she was sure, find her lacking as a supposed girlfriend of the Landris heir.

She was wearing navy blue fitted trousers, and a soft woollen jumper the same colour blue as her eyes; her hair hung loose about her shoulders, caught back from either side of her face with the two gold combs her father had given her for her twenty-first birthday. She looked smart, and tidy, but not what these people would expect, she was sure, of a "close" friend of Nathan's.

Nathan seemingly sensed her uncertainty and put a protective arm about her shoulders. 'You look beautiful,' he assured her huskily, a grin curving his sculptured mouth. 'I've kissed your lips bare of lipgloss, but apart from that—'

'Sam's right—you are a tease!' Brianna pretended to glare at him now, her eyes a deep sparkling blue, a becoming blush warming her cheeks as Nathan took the initiative and guided her out onto the terrace.

Only it wasn't the open terrace Brianna had been expecting; the area had, at some time in the last few years, been enclosed in glass, the floor carpeted and comfortable cane furniture installed, an array of pot plants adding life and colour to the elegance.

Seated around this large, enclosed area were various members of the Landris family—Susan Landris easily recognisable because of hair that was the same deep red as her daughter's. The man Brianna recognised as Roger Davis was seated next to a tall, aristocratic woman with neatly pinned blonde hair, who was obviously his wife, Clarissa, and lastly Brianna looked at Peter Landris, the shock clearly visible on his face as he looked at her, showing he hadn't added two and two together at all, nor come up with the appropriate answer—that Brianna was the female guest Nathan had decided to bring here with him for the weekend! The woman seated at his side bore a striking resemblance to Clarissa Davis, with her short blonde hair and aristocratic features, and Brianna decided she had to be Nathan's mother, Margaret, the woman who had provided the Landris son and heir and had then decided enough was enough!

Sam was right: *en masse* they were a formidable crowd, the men elegantly casual, the women, despite the fact their ages obviously ranged from fifty to over sixty, glamorously attired in designer label clothes. The jewellery that bedecked their earlobes, necks, wrists and fingers, was obviously very expensive.

'Everyone, this is Brianna,' Sam introduced excitedly, obviously enjoying the almost stunned effect Nathan and Brianna's entrance had on the rest of the family. 'Isn't that a lovely name, Mummy?' she appealed to her mother as she moved to sit on the arm of her chair. 'You and Daddy could have chosen something original like that for me,' she complained, in an obviously long-standing gripe, as her mother looked up at her affectionately. 'Especially as Daddy's middle name was Brian.'

Brianna stiffened at Nathan's side, her breath seeming to catch in her throat—and stay there. James Landris's middle name had been Brian?

Neither Nathan or his father had mentioned that fact on any of the occasions when she had seen them this last week. Nathan's only comment, if she remembered correctly, had been that her name sounded masculine...

Or a variation of a man's name...

Or a man's middle name...!

A specific man. Nathan's uncle—James Landris!

CHAPTER SIX

'DON'T jump to conclusions,' Nathan rasped. The two of them were upstairs in the bedroom Brianna had been assigned for her stay over the weekend, Nathan having taken one look at her pale, accusing face a few minutes ago and excused them both on the basis they both needed to freshen up after their journey, before tea was served.

'Don't jump to conclusions?' she repeated angrily. 'Your uncle's middle name was Brian, and you didn't even think to mention the fact!' She looked at him accusingly.

'My middle name is Samuel, after my grandfather,' Nathan sighed, sitting down wearily on the bed. 'And I didn't think to mention that, either!'

'It hardly has the same significance as Brian, does it?' she returned disgustedly, pacing the lemon and cream room, too agitated to sit down herself.

'It's purely circumstantial, Brianna,' he began soothingly. 'I didn't think—'

'Don't talk to me as if the two of us are in a courtroom, Nathan,' she cut in scathingly.

'Then don't be so damned quick to condemn a man who isn't even alive to defend himself!' he returned coldly.

'I'm not condemning anyone—'

'Aren't you?' Nathan bit out scornfully. 'It seems to me that you are. You find out, quite accidentally, that my uncle's middle name was Brian, and—wham!—he has to be the man that fathered Rebecca's baby!'

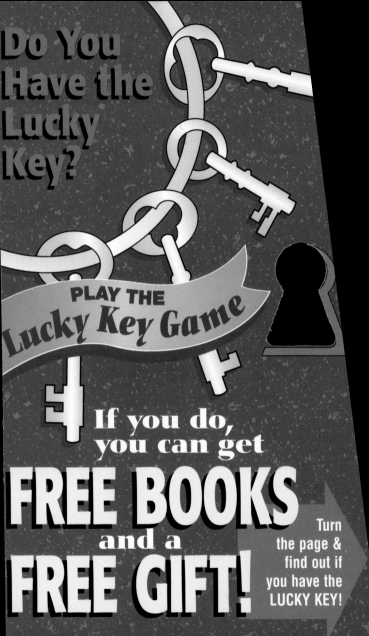

PLAY THE
Lucky Key Game
and get

HOW TO PLAY:

1. With a coin, carefully scratch off gold area at the right. Then check the claim chart to see what we have for you — **FREE BOOKS** and a **FREE GIFT** — **ALL YOURS FREE!**

2. Send back this card and you'll receive brand-new Harlequin Presents® novels. These books have a cover price of $4.25 each, but they are yours to keep absolutely free.

3. There's no catch. You're under no obligation to buy anything. We charge nothing — ZERO — for your first shipment. And you don't have to make any minimum number of purchases — not even one!

4. The fact is thousands of readers enjoy receiving books by mail from the Harlequin Reader Service® months before they're available in stores. They like the convenience of home delivery and they love our discount prices!

5. We hope that after receiving your free books you'll want to remain a subscriber. But the choice is yours — to continue or cancel, any time at all! So why not take us up on our invitation, with no risk of any kind. You'll be glad you did!

YOURS FREE!
A SURPRISE MYSTERY GIFT

We can't tell you what it is...but we're sure you'll like it! A FREE GIFT— **just for playing the LUCKY KEY game!**

FREE GIFTS!

PLAY THE
Lucky Key Game

Scratch gold area with a coin.
Then check below to see the gifts you get!

DETACH AND MAIL CARD TODAY!

YES! I have scratched off the gold area. Please send me all the gifts for which I qualify. I understand I am under no obligation to purchase any books, as explained on the back and on the opposite page.

306 HDL CH9U

Name
(PLEASE PRINT CLEARLY)

Address _____ Apt.#

City _____ Prov. _____ Postal Code

2 free books plus a mystery gift	1 free book
2 free books	Try Again!

The Harlequin Reader Service™ — Here's how it works:

Accepting free books places you under no obligation to buy anything. You may keep the books and gift and return the shipping statement marked "cancel." If you do not cancel, about a month later we'll send you 6 additional novels, and bill you just $3.49 each, plus 25¢ delivery per book and GST.* That's the complete price — and compared to cover prices of $4.25 each — quite a bargain! You may cancel at any time, but if you choose to continue, every month we'll send you 6 more books, which you may either purchase at the discount price...or return to us and cancel your subscription.

*Terms and prices subject to change without notice.
Canadian residents will be charged applicable provincial taxes and GST.

If offer card is missing, write to: Harlequin Reader Service, P.O. Box 609, Fort Erie, Ontario L2A 5X3

HARLEQUIN READER SERVICE
PO BOX 609
FORT ERIE ON   L2A 9Z9

0195619199-L2A5X3-BR01

Canada Post Corporation/Société canadienne des postes
Postage paid   Port payé
If mailed in Canada   si posté au Canada
Business   Réponse
Reply   d'affaires
0195619199   01

MAIL▶POSTE

'Rebecca chose my name herself, did you know that?' Brianna was undaunted. 'My adoptive father told me about it; it was something she was quite insistent upon—'

'It proves nothing, Brianna,' Nathan interrupted her. 'You've heard one fact, one minor detail, and you're building a case against my uncle on the basis of it, letting your imagination run away with you.'

'You told me yourself that Rebecca never went anywhere but to school and back home again, so isn't it logical to assume that her baby's father either lived locally, or visited often?'

'As my family obviously do!' Nathan finished scathingly. 'Taken on that criteria, every man who lived in the area comes under suspicion! Well, besides the butler you saw on your arrival, we have one other manservant in the household, three gardeners—one of whom, I believe, is also called Brian—and then there's—'

'Okay, okay, there's no need to be nasty about this,' Brianna said quickly. 'It was just a shock to hear about your uncle earlier—something completely unexpected.' Perhaps she had overreacted, she now realised. Although she still had an uneasy feeling in the pit of her stomach... 'I'm sorry if you thought I was being insulting to your uncle,' she apologised.

Nathan stood up, his expression still annoyed. 'I thought the main reason for your visit here was so that you could meet your grandfather?'

And not to hurl rash accusations at members of the Landris family, especially, as he said, one who wasn't alive to defend himself. Or otherwise... She was doing it again! She had better stop, before Nathan lost all patience with her.

'It is,' she confirmed briskly. 'Let's hope that sound doesn't carry in this house,' she added wryly, knowing that if they had been shouting at each other in this way in her own home, the whole family would have come running to see what was wrong. 'Otherwise your relatives will have heard us having an argument as soon as we've arrived!'

Nathan grasped her arm in preparation of leaving the bedroom. 'It isn't the first time we've argued—and I doubt it will be the last, either!' he added, as they walked down the wide staircase to rejoin the group.

Brianna looked at him from beneath lowered lashes. He made it sound as if their acquaintance wouldn't be at an end after this weekend was over. Unless she was just reading more into his statement than had actually been there…? Letting her imagination run away with her again!

But she was getting quite used to Nathan being a part of her life; she'd felt a rush of excitement when he'd arrived at her home earlier today to pick her up; her legs had been slightly shaky as she'd hurried to the door in answer to his ring of the bell, and a warm blush had come to her cheeks as she'd looked at him standing on the doorstep.

She was falling in love with Nathan Landris, she suddenly realised breathlessly.

Not the most sensible thing she had ever done!

In fact the opposite, in the circumstances. Until her father's identity was revealed, she didn't dare allow herself to love Nathan. What if it did turn out they were related? Nathan could be her cousin—or worse, in view of Peter Landris's intense interest in all of this…

She didn't even want to think of that possibility!

'Where have you gone off to now?' Nathan was frowning darkly as he watched the emotions flickering across her face.

'Er—I was—I was just thinking I still don't have any

lipgloss on,' Brianna hastily prevaricated. If Nathan had been angry at her feelings concerning his uncle, he would be furious if he were to know what she had been thinking just seconds ago!

He shrugged. 'The family will think I kissed it all off again.'

She arched blonde brows. 'I didn't realise you were so well known for your passion!' she taunted. Although, she admitted inwardly, the Ice Man was fast fading from her memory!

'Nathan is the proverbial iceberg, aren't you, cuz?' put in the easily recognisable voice of Samantha Landris. 'One tenth visible on the ocean's surface, the other nine-tenths hidden from view!'

Brianna laughed huskily, finding the remark funny, since it followed so closely on her own thoughts.

'When the two of you have quite finished...?' Nathan drawled dryly.

Sam grinned at him unrepentantly. 'I was sent to get you for tea; you've been gone quite long enough as far as Aunt Margaret is concerned!'

'Was she sent or did she volunteer?' Nathan muttered to Brianna as the two of them followed Sam out to the terrace conservatory.

'Oh, I volunteered.' Sam turned back to grin at them cheekily. 'Aunt Margaret would have been deeply shocked if she'd found the two of you in a compromising position. I think she tried sex once and didn't like it!' she added confidingly to Brianna.

'Sam!' Nathan hissed reprovingly.

'Oh, all right, perhaps it was twice—just to reassure herself she wasn't wrong about the first time!' Sam grinned wickedly. 'Not that Aunt Margaret is ever wrong about anything,' she added with a grimace.

Brianna could see that although Nathan found his

cousin's outrageousness disarming, he also found her amusing, holding back his smile with effort. And she had to admit Sam was a breath of fresh air in what was otherwise turning out to be a very staid weekend party.

Peter Landris was stiffly polite as they all had tea, and she found his wife Margaret equally as coolly aloof as she dispensed the tea cups. The Davises both following their lead, with only Susan Landris proving to be as bright and bubbly as her daughter, if a little subdued by the present company.

Brianna felt as if they were all looking at her as a potential bride for Nathan—which, in the circumstances, was understandable—and finding her wanting! Having made sure Nathan was her only child, Margaret Landris seemed the most critical, watching Brianna's every move, it seemed. She had obviously hoped for better things for her only son, the Landris heir.

'I was wondering why it is that you seem so familiar...' Roger Davis murmured as he strolled over to join her as she drank her cup of tea, a short, grey-haired man, the severity of his features softened by the warm blue of his eyes.

She looked up at him guardedly, wishing Nathan was still at her side. But his mother had temporarily captured his attention—was probably even now asking him where on earth he had met someone like Brianna! 'Oh?' she returned noncommittally. Not another one who recognised her as Rebecca's daughter!

He nodded. 'I believe I may have seen you at the office one lunchtime earlier this week. With Nathan?' he added questioningly.

Of course; he had walked by that day when she and Nathan were leaving the office. 'I remember,' she acknowledged with a polite smile, aware that his wife was watching them with narrowed eyes from across the room.

'Have the two of you—known each other long?' he continued conversationally.

Brianna looked at him from beneath dark lashes, suddenly having the feeling that this man was asking someone else's questions for her—namely his sister-in-law. She also had a feeling that, in spite of his business partnership with Peter Landris, this man knew nothing about Rebecca's will, or Brianna's connection with it...

'A while,' she prevaricated. 'We're really only friends,' she added dismissively. 'Nathan just thought I would enjoy a weekend in the country.'

'With all his family?' Roger derided, blue eyes twinkling with amusement. 'This family has been likened to a pack of wolves, my dear; I hardly think Nathan would have exposed you to us on a whim!'

'As one of the wolves, he's probably enjoying my discomfort,' she returned wittily.

Roger Davis laughed. 'I have a feeling you very rarely feel discomforted, my dear.' He smiled warmly, obviously relaxing in her company.

She raised blonde brows. 'Nathan has caused me the odd moment,' she admitted.

He glanced across the room to where his nephew was now in conversation with Susan Landris. 'Nathan is a wonderful man. And an excellent lawyer. He's a person to be proud of.'

Brianna felt a flush of pleasure at his admiration of the man she had so recently discovered she was falling in love with. 'Could it be that the "wonderful man" and "excellent lawyer" are sometimes at war with each other...?'

The older man's gaze returned to her. 'In Nathan's case, no.'

Brianna didn't know what else to say. She was rapidly coming to the conclusion herself that Nathan was a wonderful man, so what else *was* there to say?

'I didn't mean to embarrass you, my dear.' Roger Davis lightly touched her shoulder. 'My intention was to put you at your ease, not the contrary!'

She smiled up at him, deciding he was quite a nice man—perhaps even a little of an outsider himself in this pack of wolves…? Although surely, as Peter Landris's partner, and married to Peter's wife's sister, he shouldn't be.

'Do you have children, Mr Davis?' Just because they weren't here, it didn't mean that Nathan didn't have other cousins besides the effervescent Sam.

'Two Old English Sheepdogs called Peg and Danny,' he returned dryly. 'Of course those aren't their pedigree names, but to us at home they're Peg and Danny. My wife shows them,' he explained lightly.

Brianna wondered if their lack of children was because Clarissa shared similar feelings to those of her older sister; obviously Clarissa Davis preferred dogs to children! Perhaps dogs were easier to deal with. Looking at Clarissa Davis now, as she crossed the room to join Roger and herself, Brianna observed a coldly aristocratic woman, so it wasn't too difficult to believe!

'Darling, you're monopolising Nathan's guest,' she playfully reproved her husband as she reached his side.

'I was glad of the company, Mrs Davis,' Brianna assured her.

Some of the hardness seemed to leave the beautifully sculptured face, Clarissa's smile appearing genuine as she looked down at Brianna. 'I'm afraid it's always a bit frantic at these weekend get-togethers when Sam chooses to put in an appearance.' She gave an affectionately exasperated look across the room to where Sam seemed to be entertaining her mother and Nathan with an exaggerated mime of some poor unfortunate person. 'Although I must say,' Clarissa confessed softly, 'she does tend to liven things up!'

Brianna couldn't contain her laugh at the obvious relief in the older woman's voice. Obviously Clarissa Davis did have a sense of humour after all, leading Brianna to reassess her first impression that Clarissa was rather remote. Taking into account her own changed feelings towards Nathan, she had to admit that her first impressions of this family were maybe slightly wrong! Although she had yet to actually speak to Margaret Landris, Nathan's mother...

'Sam is an actress,' Roger Davis supplied.

'Our black sheep,' Clarissa confirmed ruefully.

Brianna glanced across the room at the young redhead, easily able to visualise that vibrant personality totally dominating the stage with her presence. She didn't doubt for a moment that if Sam had chosen to be an actress, then she was a good one. Black sheep or not, she was a Landris, after all!

'Every family has one,' she lightly answered the older couple.

'Lord, yes!' Clarissa grinned—and it totally transformed her face. The aristocratic coldness was gone, her face now appearing youthfully mischievous; Clarissa Davis was beautiful! In her early fifties, as was her husband, that height and cool blondeness gave her a remoteness that could be deceptive. 'Believe it or not—' she draped her arm companionably through her husband's '—I was always in trouble when Margaret and I were young.'

'She married me—that was trouble!' Roger put in humorously.

His wife gave a tinkling laugh. 'That isn't true, and

you know it. You were my redemption in my parents' eyes. They were in total despair—'

'My ears were burning just now,' Sam interrupted cheerfully as she joined their group, Nathan at her side.

'Come and say hello properly to my parents.' Nathan gently grasped Brianna's arm as she stood up.

'There, I said we were monopolising you.' Clarissa apologised.

'Not at all,' Brianna assured her, starting to feel a little dizzy from the jumble of personalities in the room. None of them was as they appeared to be! But then, neither was she, she realised guiltily... 'I would love to meet your parents,' she told Nathan warmly.

'What did you do to Aunt Clarissa?' Nathan whispered as they crossed the terrace together.

She gave him a startled look. 'I thought she was very nice,' she defended.

'She seemed quite taken with you too,' he observed.

Brianna turned away; of course, her getting on with his family, and them liking her, wasn't in his plan for this weekend! 'I'm sorry,' she murmured.

Nathan came to a halt, not seeming to care that they were now standing in the middle of the terrace, surrounded by his curious relatives. 'What on earth are you sorry about?'

'I'm beginning to realise what a bad idea this was. It's as I told you earlier—they all assume I'm your girlfriend, and—'

'And you're starting to feel guilty because it isn't true,' Nathan guessed easily.

'I like them, Nathan.' Her eyes flashed deeply blue in her agitation. 'I feel a fraud. It isn't in my nature to deceive people.'

'Then don't deceive them.' He bent down and lightly brushed his lips over hers. 'After all, I've taken you out to dinner,' he said huskily, 'kissed you—argued with you,' he added wryly. 'That's as close to being a girl-friend as you can get!'

Not exactly! The thought of actually being Nathan's girlfriend frightened her more than the pretence had!

'Let's go and say hello to your parents,' she muttered as she continued across the room, aware that Nathan was chuckling behind her.

Margaret Landris appeared to have none of the under-lying softness that Brianna had just discovered in her younger sister; she was obviously a strong force within the family, despite the success of her husband and son. As Brianna was discovering all too strongly, anyone who didn't have a rather overpowering strength of character was likely to be swallowed up and spat out again by this family. She was starting to feel exhausted just from meeting them all.

'How did the two of you get together?' Margaret Landris enquired coolly.

How did they get together? How on earth could two such different people as herself and Nathan possibly have hooked up?

'Brianna came to the office on a legal matter,' Nathan replied smoothly. 'I took the opportunity of asking her out.'

The truth. Of course. And, because Peter Landris didn't discuss his work with his wife, Margaret would have no idea what that legal matter had been about! Clever Nathan...

'I see,' his mother said frostily, still looking down her aristocratic nose at Brianna. 'I wasn't sure whether or not you were the daughter of one of our acquaintances; you somehow seem familiar...?'

Peter Landris, Nathan, and Brianna all seemed to hold their breath at the same time, Brianna looking up at the older woman with widely apprehensive eyes. Both Nathan and his father had known exactly who she was the moment they saw her, so it was a distinct possibility someone else in the family might make the same connection! Although Nathan and his father had had the knowledge of her existence and her visit to their office to help them... But, even so...

'I just can't place you.' Margaret Landris frowned her irritation with herself.

And the three people standing with her all started to breathe again!

'Nathan tells me your father is an obstetrician, Brianna,' the older woman continued conversationally.

'That's right, he is.' She nodded, relieved to change the subject. And perhaps her father's profession would prove acceptable to this woman!

'Brianna's father is a specialist in his field, with his own private practice,' Nathan supplied, raising his brows mockingly at Brianna as she looked up at him in surprise; she hadn't realised he knew so much about her or her family!

'How nice,' Margaret Landris looked suitably impressed. 'So much better to be dealing with the beginning of life rather than the end of it!'

As Brianna knew only too well, though, from the few times her father had returned home in despair, that wasn't always the case. But she could see that Nathan knew exactly how to deal with his mother, that he had, in fact, appealed to the snobbish side of her nature. He knew his mother very well indeed!

'How true,' Brianna agreed dryly.

'I thought I might take Brianna for a swim,' Nathan put in briskly. 'We have plenty of time before dinner.'

Brianna looked at him in alarm now. A swim? 'I haven't brought my swimsuit with me.'

'Sam always leaves a costume or two about the place.' Nathan easily dealt with her objection. 'I'm sure we'll be able to find you something to wear.'

'That sounds lovely,' she accepted. She was quite happy to escape any further grilling from Margaret Landris for the moment, and relax for a couple of hours.

This was all proving much more difficult than she could ever have imagined. All her attention had been focused on meeting her grandfather; she hadn't really given too much thought to the time she would spend with Nathan's family. Although she *was* finding—with the exception of his mother, who she found as cool and distant as she had imagined she might be—that she actually liked them—and that was making everything more difficult, not easier!

Nathan cupped a firm hand under her elbow. 'We'll see you all later at dinner.'

Peter Landris hadn't spoken a word, and he didn't now, although he still frowned darkly as the two of them left the room together.

'Your father is worried,' Brianna told Nathan once they were out in the wide hallway.

Nathan shrugged. 'I can't help that.'

'You didn't have to bring me here,' she reasoned.

He looked down at her with raised brows. 'Didn't I?'

'Nathan—'

'Brianna, will you stop worrying about other people so much?' he admonished. 'My father is old enough to take care of himself.'

She wasn't so sure about that; Peter Landris had looked sick from the moment she had entered the terrace area with Nathan. But if Nathan, his own son, wasn't concerned about that, then perhaps he was right, and she shouldn't worry so much.

'Where are you going?' Nathan asked as she turned to go up the stairs.

She paused. 'To get my jacket. It's a bit cooler outside now.'

'Brianna, the pool is inside, at the back of the house,' he explained patiently. 'We aren't going out.'

The Landris home had its own indoor swimming pool. Of course it did. Didn't everyone's!

'You're a great leveller, Brianna,' Nathan told her as he saw her expression. 'I never even think about how lucky we are to have our own pool,' he explained as she rejoined him at the bottom of the staircase. 'It's just always been there.'

And very nice it was too, as Brianna discovered a few minutes later. Like the terrace, it was completely enclosed, the floor-to-ceiling windows looking out over the beautiful gardens at the back of the house, where blazes of spring flowers gave bright patches of colour and the lawns were green and smooth, appearing as if they had been freshly mown. Probably by one of the three gardeners Nathan said his parents employed!

'My mother likes to do the flowerbeds herself,' Nathan told her, seeming once again to guess her thoughts.

'It all looks lovely.' Brianna turned away from the magnificent view and gazed at the huge swimming pool in which the water was crystal-clear; it was surrounded by marble tiles and an abundance of exotic flowers and plants that flourished in the heated room. 'Where will I find a costume?' She couldn't quite look at Nathan now, the differences between them seeming to grow wider by the minute.

Nathan put a restraining hand on her arm. 'Brianna...?'

She looked up at him, once again feeling that jolt of

awareness as she looked into his austerely handsome face. She was falling in love with this man—and he was way out of her reach!

He looked at her searchingly. 'Brianna.' He spoke softly. 'This is my parents' home. I have a home in town.'

Her mouth twisted wryly. 'And it's probably as luxurious as this!'

He smiled, shaking his head. 'I'll show it to you some time. I think you might be pleasantly surprised. One thing growing up in a show-house like this, rather than a home, does for you is to make damned sure you don't live anywhere remotely like it when you're old enough to have a place of your own!'

He had piqued her curiosity now. She had imagined him living in a super-modern flat, all chrome and black furniture, with *objets d'art* adorning the shiny surfaces. Nathan seemed to be saying she had imagined it completely wrongly!

'The bedroom you've been given for your stay here used to be my nursery, Brianna,' he continued. 'It adjoins my bedroom, you see. They were the only two rooms I was allowed to play in when I was a child.'

She frowned as another image came into her mind, that of a lonely little boy, upstairs in his nursery, probably in the care of a nanny. It was in stark contrast to her own boisterous childhood, with a lively younger brother and parents believing very strongly that children should be seen as well as heard. Maybe there were disadvantages to a so-called privileged background that she hadn't even thought of...

'Don't feel sorry for me, Brianna.' Nathan grinned suddenly. 'In spite of that, I got into all sorts of boyhood scrapes!'

Fishing, playing cricket and climbing trees, she remembered. With Rebecca...

'I'm sure you did,' Brianna acknowledged huskily. After all, he had acquired that devilish grin from somewhere!

'Let's go and have that swim,' he suggested. 'You'll find some of Sam's things in the changing-room, I'm sure.'

Brianna was glad of the diversion. Because something else he had said had just registered in her head: her bedroom adjoined his...!

She very much doubted that this was accidental; obviously his mother had done her own share of adding up—and had come to her own conclusion about her son's relationship with Brianna.

She couldn't help wondering if Nathan's ex-fiancée had occupied that bedroom, too, when she came to stay...

The water was absolutely glorious, beautifully warm, which was probably as well because Brianna had run out of the changing-room to jump straight into the water. This was because the things of Sam's she had found in the changing-room consisted of two strips of black material that barely covered what they were supposed to! Brianna had felt almost naked once she had the triangular bits of material in place, and the only solution to her embarrassment seemed to be to get into the water and hide the skimpiness of the costume as soon as possible.

'Good dive,' Nathan told her as she surfaced beside him some seconds later, shaking the water from her eyes as she pushed the hair back from her face. 'And an even better body,' he added, laughing softly as she blushed. 'Sam always was an exhibitionist!'

So much for jumping in the water quickly so that she wouldn't be seen; Nathan must have been treading water just waiting for her entrance!

They discovered over the next hour that she was almost as strong a swimmer as he was, and when the time came to get out of the water she did so unselfconsciously; she had never felt awkward about her body before, knowing she was tiny but shapely. And Nathan had obviously liked what he'd seen earlier!

What she wasn't prepared for, as they stepped out of the pool together, was how lithely attractive Nathan looked in navy blue swimming trunks, his hair damp and lightly curly, giving him that rakish appearance she found so disturbing.

'What is it?' Nathan asked her as she stared at him. 'What's wrong?'

She couldn't breathe!

This was ridiculous. Just looking at a man shouldn't take her breath away. But this wasn't just any man; he was Nathan. And she wasn't falling in love with him at all; she'd already done so!

'Brianna!' he said sharply at her continued silence. 'You're very pale. Don't you feel well?'

She felt altogether too well, that was the problem. Wasn't her life complicated enough at the moment, without adding her love for Nathan to it?

'I think a lie-down before dinner wouldn't come amiss,' she replied. 'I'm a little—over-emotional.' That had to be the understatement of the year! She wanted Nathan, found him so physically exciting she was shaking.

He draped his arm concernedly about her naked shoulders. 'God, you're trembling,' he said worriedly. 'You should have told me—I should have thought. You always give the impression you're so damned self-assured,

I never thought about what an ordeal all of this was going to be for you.' He shook his head self-disgustedly. 'Go and change, and then I'll show you the way back to your bedroom. And if you don't feel better after your rest, I'll bring dinner up to you on a tray.'

He had completely misconstrued the reason for her trembling—thank goodness! The poor man would probably run a mile if he realised how she felt about him. He had his life all mapped out, and his career, he didn't need someone like her coming along and complicating his life, either.

She smiled bravely. 'I don't think that will be necessary, thank you, Nathan. A little rest, and I'll be fine again.' As soon as she put some distance between them she would start to feel better!

He nodded. 'If you're sure...?' He still looked concerned.

'I'm sure,' she confirmed, just wanting to get away from the seductive intimacy of this situation.

'Okay.' He bent his head and kissed her lightly on the lips. 'I could quite get used to this,' he murmured as he held her body and gently moulded it against his.

Well, she couldn't—she had just stopped breathing again!

'I wouldn't, Nathan.' She stepped firmly away from him. 'This will all be over soon, and then there will be no reason for us to see each other again. Don't worry about taking me back to my bedroom; I can remember the way,' she said hastily, turning and walking away—before she lost her nerve completely and just melted into his arms, lost herself in the warm intimacy of his body as she longed to do.

She didn't glance back, but she could sense him watching her, deliberately not hurrying to the changing-room. Although once she reached there the trembling started again, and she had to sit down on the bench seat before her knees gave away.

Once this weekend was over she had to stay well away from Nathan. And, loving him as she did, that might hurt, though surely not any more than it did now.

Her heart leapt erratically when a knock sounded on her bedroom door some time later. She couldn't cope with seeing Nathan again just yet!

'Brianna?'

She instantly recognised the cool, aristocratic voice of Nathan's mother. Margaret Landris! What could she possibly want to see her about?

Her expression was wary as she opened the door and faced the older woman. 'Yes?'

Margaret smiled, but somehow it didn't quite reach her eyes. 'Nathan tells me you aren't feeing too well. I wondered if I could get you anything?'

'It's nothing.' Brianna shrugged dismissively.

'Nathan seemed quite concerned,' the older woman persisted.

Nathan had probably been irritated by his mother's interest. 'I'm just tired,' she assured the other woman. 'And I wanted to be fresh for dinner this evening.'

'Nathan seems—quite taken with you,' his mother ventured.

And this woman wanted to know just how 'taken' Brianna was with her Nathan! 'We're just friends,' Brianna replied, although she had a feeling that wouldn't lull Margaret's worries concerning her son; Nathan wasn't the type of man to bring home just a 'friend' to meet his family.

Well, there was nothing Brianna could say to comfort Margaret Landris. The truth certainly wouldn't do!

'I see,' the older woman said slowly. 'Well, do let me

know if there's anything I can get for you.' She spoke as the polite hostess now.

'I will. Thank you.' Brianna nodded, closing the door with some relief, knowing that any woman who took on Nathan would have to be brave enough to take on his mother too—thank God she didn't have a chance with him!

'Your mother doesn't like me,' Brianna stated abruptly.

'What?' Nathan glared at her, checking in his determined stride up the driveway.

Brianna sighed, continuing to walk at his side, the gravel stones crunching beneath their feet. 'I said, your mother doesn't like me,' she repeated patiently. 'Did she like your fiancée?' she asked interestedly.

'Brianna—'

'Probably not,' she thoughtfully answered her own question. 'Your mother is very possessive of you, Nathan.' As had been proved at dinner the evening before. As hostess, Margaret Landris must have been in charge of the seating arrangements, and so she had sat Brianna at the other end of the table from Nathan, between Samantha and Roger Davis. Not that she was complaining about her dinner companions, they had both proved to be great fun, but the distance placed between herself and Nathan hadn't been lost on her.

'I'm really not interested in my mother at this moment in time, Brianna,' Nathan barked. 'And neither should you be. I meant what I said the other day—I hope you aren't expecting miracles where your grandfather is concerned, because I can tell you now, Giles is still as hard as he ever was. More so, probably, sitting alone in that big house with nothing but his memories.'

The big house in question came into view now, as the two of them took a Sunday morning walk, as Nathan had promised they would. The Mallory house was nowhere near as well-kept as the Landris home; the driveway and garden looked overgrown, and the house itself, a huge grey-stoned monstrosity, sadly neglected.

Brianna gave no answer as they continued to walk up the gravel driveway. She had dressed casually for their walk, in a cropped blue jumper and black denims matched with black ankle boots. She wasn't too sure it was an outfit a man of seventy would approve of, especially a forbidding one, but she really didn't care. She wasn't here to impress Giles Mallory; she merely wanted to know if Brianna had ever told him the identity of her baby's father!

'Brianna—'

'Will you stop worrying, Nathan?' she told him impatiently. 'I'm not here for any last-minute acts of forgiveness. Besides,' she added sharply, 'Giles Mallory will probably seem quite tame after almost twenty-four hours in the company of your family!'

Nathan's relatives were obviously close, otherwise they wouldn't spend time together, but, nevertheless, they were all very distinct personalities too, and with the mischievous Sam there to act as chief stirrer, the meal the evening before had turned into a heated debate about one subject after another. Brianna had just sat back and watched them in the end, deciding it wasn't so different from home after all; where usually Gary liked to stir things up. God help them all, Brianna had decided, if Sam and Gary should ever be in the same room together!

Nathan pulled a face. 'I did warn you about Sam.'

But he hadn't warned her about his mother... Once or twice Margaret Landris had tried to draw Brianna into the conversation, solely for the reason of talking her down, Brianna had decided. And on that basis she had been noncommittal on every subject that came up.

Margaret Landris had probably decided she was a completely wishy-washy character, but if that made this visit easier to get through, Brianna was happy to let her go on thinking it.

'I think Sam's wonderful!'

'She can't differentiate between being on stage and off it!' Nathan exclaimed disgustedly. 'She plays to the audience either way!'

Brianna spluttered with laughter. 'She managed to annoy you a couple of times last night.' Quite a lot, as she remembered.

'She manages to annoy everyone.' He scowled.

'She didn't annoy me.' Brianna still smiled, although she knew that Nathan was chatting away like this to take her mind off the fact they were fast approaching the Mallory house. And she was happy to let him do so; her nerves were strung out to breaking point.

He raised dark brows. 'She doesn't know you well enough yet. Give her time!'

Brianna sobered. There wouldn't be any time for Sam to get to know her. This weekend was it.

Nathan put a hand lightly on her arm. 'Let me handle this, initially, okay?' he said as they approached the heavy oak front door of the house. 'Burns, the butler, knows me.'

She allowed him to go forward in front of her. 'Whatever it takes to get inside.'

He drew in a deeply controlling breath before ringing the doorbell. 'Burns is almost as old as Giles, so this could take a while,' he explained.

It did, and the man who finally opened the door seemed as bent and creaky as the door itself!

He squinted up at Nathan from the darkness of the hallway. 'Is that you, Mr Nathan?' The butler's voice was as rusty as the hinges on the door, which had squeaked when he opened it!

'I want to see Mr Giles, Burns.' Nathan raised his voice—the butler was obviously deaf, as well as bent with age.

The butler slowly shook his head. 'It's not a good day, Mr Nathan,' he advised worriedly. 'I don't—'

'Will you please go and tell Mr Mallory that he has two visitors to see him?' Brianna put in firmly. She had no intention of being turned away at the door, especially as this whole scene was starting to take on the ridiculousness of a farce!

The elderly man squinted at her too now, a puzzled frown settling on his lined brow. 'And who might you be, miss?'

'My name is Gibson,' was all she supplied.

'Please tell Mr Giles we're here, Burns,' Nathan said wearily, turning back to Brianna once the butler had shuffled off in search of his employer. 'So much for leaving it to me,' he protested.

'He was going to turn us away,' she said unrepentantly. 'And I want to see Rebecca's father.'

Nathan gave a heavy sigh. 'I've never thought coming here was a good idea.' He shook his head. 'You don't—'

'Mr Giles will see you both in the library.' The butler had shuffled back so quietly neither of them had been aware of him; he seemed almost surprised himself at his employer's acquiescence, obviously having expected a quite different response to their request.

The library turned out to be a room lined with dusty-looking books that didn't look as if they had been read for centuries, with worn chairs on a threadbare carpet and a meagre fire burning in the grate adding little warmth to the chill of the room.

'A few more cobwebs and it could be *Great*

Expectations all over again!' Brianna muttered to Nathan, wondering how on earth anyone could live in such discomfort, let alone an old man.

'Except I'm not Miss Havisham and you aren't Pip,' rasped a derisive voice. A man sitting forward on one of the high wing-backed chairs that flanked the fireplace looked across the room at the two of them. 'And there's nothing wrong with my hearing, either!'

Brianna stared at the man who was her maternal grandfather, not knowing quite what she had expected, except that he wasn't it!

He was a farmer's son, and she had somehow expected him to be short and stocky, very bald, with a ruddy complexion, but the man who now slowly stood up was easily as tall as Nathan, very thin, his thick hair snowy white and his haughty-looking face not in the least ruddy. Although the tweed suit he wore was old and worn, he wore it with an arrogant bearing that dismissed such things as unimportant. Formidable, Brianna decided...

'We're sorry to interrupt you, Giles,' Nathan said politely as the other man bent to put down on a side-table the book he had obviously been reading when they had arrived.

'You might be, Nathan,' Giles Mallory grated in reply to the apology, his narrow-eyed gaze never leaving Brianna's pale face. 'But I doubt that missy here is,' he said knowingly. 'Not what you expected, am I?' he added with satisfaction.

She swallowed hard, a little dazed by his obvious attack. 'I—I'm not sure what I expected.' She shook her head.

'I'm not sure what I was expecting, either.' He stepped forward, immediately dominating, looking

Brianna slowly up and down before nodding his head. 'You look like your mother,' he pronounced hardly.

Brianna stared at him. 'You—know—who—I—am...?'

'Of course I know who you are,' he growled impatiently. 'Did you think I wouldn't recognise my own granddaughter?'

He knew who she was!

CHAPTER SEVEN

BRIANNA stared at him. She couldn't do anything else. He knew exactly who she was. How did he know? And why didn't he, in the circumstances, seem angry or upset at her presence here? She didn't understand this. This certainly wasn't what she had been expecting!

'Cat got your tongue, girl?' he snapped at her strained silence.

'Giles—'

'I'm talking to my granddaughter, Nathan,' the older man stated tersely as Nathan started to speak.

'I understand that, Giles,' Nathan soothed. 'But Brianna is a little—shaken.'

'Can't understand why she should be.' The older man turned to pull a bell that would obviously summon the butler. 'She's the one that came to see me, not the other way round. Burns.' He turned to the butler as he appeared in the doorway behind Brianna. 'Bring coffee for three,' he instructed abruptly. 'I take it you do drink coffee?' he prompted Brianna gruffly. 'Only your mother couldn't stand it.'

'I—drink coffee.' She nodded. 'I—would you mind if I sat down?' She frowned at the effort of staying on her feet. She had been completely thrown by this man's reaction to her presence here, still couldn't even begin to understand it.

'Of course you can sit down,' Giles Mallory answered irritably. 'You haven't come all this way to stand in the doorway. Besides, you'll be in Burns' way when he comes back with the coffee things.' He turned to Nathan. 'Parents both well, Nathan?'

Nathan looked as nonplussed as Brianna felt. 'Er—my parents are very well, thank you.'

'Good, good.' The older man nodded briefly before looking back at Brianna. 'Feeling better yet, girl?'

She wasn't sure what she was feeling! She had come here expecting to hate this man, had despised him before she even met him. And yet, face to face with him...

'I never could stand chattering females, anyway.' He sat down in the chair opposite Brianna, near the fire. 'Find yourself a seat, Nathan,' he barked. 'And stop making the place look untidy.'

Brianna knew the remark would have been funny if she hadn't been feeling quite so stunned; every available surface was cluttered with books, and dust covered all of them. Nathan's neat appearance, in black trousers and a cream-coloured shirt, could in no way add to the untidiness of the room. Nevertheless, Nathan did as he was invited, removing several books from a chair before sitting down, a short distance away.

'Stop looking as if you're about to get up and take flight,' Giles Mallory rasped as Brianna fidgeted restlessly. 'I'm not about to start ranting and raving at you like a demented idiot. Despite what you may have been told to the contrary...' He gave Nathan a pointed look.

'I didn't—'

'Nathan hasn't told me much about you at all,' Brianna calmly defended, some of her equilibrium returning. Thank goodness!

The older man gave a wicked grin. 'He told you enough that he felt he should come with you today—just in case!'

Brianna stared across at him. 'You're enjoying this, aren't you...?' she realised.

'Of course I'm enjoying it. Waited long enough for it, haven't I?' Giles informed her scathingly.

'Long enough for what?' She still stared at him. She couldn't work out what this man was up to at all, whether or not he was playing some sort of cat and mouse game with them...

'To meet my granddaughter, of course,' he snapped.

She shook her head. 'How could you possibly know I would ever come here?'

He raised snowy brows. 'Well, if you didn't, then you don't have any of Rebecca's spirit in you. She never ran away from anything in her life!'

'She ran away from you,' Brianna reminded him harshly.

He became suddenly still, his eyes narrowed. 'Is that what you were told?' he said.

'It's what happened,' Brianna returned forcefully.

He met her gaze steadily. 'Is it?'

She looked at him searchingly, unnerved by his stillness. 'Isn't it?' she said slowly.

'Not exactly,' he replied gravely. 'Not completely. Ah, here's Burns with the coffee,' he said as the clatter of cups on a tray could be heard before the elderly butler even entered the room.

Giles stood up, removing a pile of books from the table next to Brianna, shifting them unceremoniously onto the floor.

Brianna watched him. He wasn't what she had expected, either. Rather than the cantankerous despot she had been expecting, she was starting to see him as a rather lonely old man. Obviously a situation of his own making, but that didn't make it any less true.

The elderly butler staggered in with the laden tray, Nathan leaping up to take it from him as Burns looked in danger of dropping the whole lot onto the floor.

Accompanying the coffee-pot and cups were homemade biscuits, and plates, so there was obviously a cook in the house somewhere. It just seemed to be the housekeeping itself that left something to be desired...

'Pour the coffee, then, girl,' Giles instructed briskly, once the butler had left.

'My name is Brianna,' she told him firmly before lifting the coffeepot.

'I'm well aware of your name. I'll have some of those biscuits too.'

'*Please,*' she responded.

His mouth twisted. 'So, you do have some of your mother in you. Your grandmother too, if I'm not mistaken. Now there was a real lady,' he added warmly as Brianna handed him the coffee and biscuits.

Maybe time had mellowed him, softened him—and his memories!—because he certainly wasn't coming across to Brianna as the tyrannical despot she had imagined.

'Thank you for the coffee and biscuits,' he accepted grudgingly.

'You're welcome,' she returned almost as grudgingly.

Giles grinned across at Nathan. 'So what do you think of my granddaughter, lad?'

Nathan looked decidedly uncomfortable at the question. 'Er—she has spirit, Giles.'

'Beautiful too, eh,' the older man prompted mischievously.

Nathan glanced across at Brianna, his smile gentle at her obvious discomfort. 'Very,' he agreed huskily.

Giles nodded his satisfaction with Nathan's answer. 'What did your family make of her?'

'I—'

'Don't answer that, Nathan,' Brianna said crossly, as she handed him his coffee and biscuits, turning back to pick up her own coffee cup before sitting down again. 'We didn't come here to answer a lot of questions,' she told the older man firmly.

'It was your intention to ask them, hmm?' he replied shrewdly. 'Well, one, anyway,' he added, his voice faltering a little.

Brianna looked at him sharply, her eyes narrowed. 'And which question would that be?' she asked warily.

Giles's mouth firmed into a thin line. 'The same question I asked your mother before she ran away. The question that was the reason she ran away,' he amended harshly. 'Who was your father?'

'And did she answer you?' Brianna held her breath.

'Of course she didn't answer me,' he snapped viciously, standing up impatiently. 'Why the hell do you think she ran away?'

'Giles—'

'It's all right, Nathan,' Brianna assured him. 'Why don't you tell us that?' she said as she turned back to Giles Mallory.

'I just did.' He glared at her from beneath bushy white brows. 'I wanted to know who the baby's father was— your father. Rebecca refused to name him. We argued. She left.' He spoke more quietly now, unemotionally.

'Why didn't you try to bring her back?' Brianna accused. 'She was only eighteen. Completely alone, and pregnant!'

'Do you think I wasn't well aware of that, girl?' he returned with cold fury. 'Rebecca didn't want me to find her. Didn't want anyone to find her. She changed her name. I had people looking for her for weeks—'

'Why?' Brianna challenged. 'Exactly why did you want to bring her back here?'

'Not for the reason you're thinking!' His eyes were narrowed to icy slits. 'Don't come here nearly twenty-two years later with your preconceived ideas, Brianna,' he told her angrily. 'You didn't know any of us then—and you still don't. And as for you, boy—' he looked across at Nathan '—you only know what you've been told. And things are not always what they seem. I may have seemed like an overbearing tyrant when you were a boy, but you didn't know—' He broke off, his face suddenly ashen as he drew in a sharply rasping breath before dropping down into the chair behind him.

'What is it?' Brianna moved forward, concern etched into her own pale features.

'Giles?' Nathan was at the older man's side now. 'Giles, what is it?'

'Pills,' Giles managed to gasp out, his hands tightly gripping the arms of the chair as he bent forward in obvious pain. 'Find Burns. He knows what to do.'

Brianna remembered now what the aged butler had said about it not being a good day when they arrived. If she wasn't mistaken, Giles Mallory had some sort of heart condition.

'I'll go,' she said briskly as she stood up. 'Loosen his collar, Nathan, and make sure he stays calm.'

'There speaks a doctor's daughter,' Giles muttered dryly as she hurried from the room.

How did he know her adoptive father was a doctor? Brianna shook her head dismissively; Giles Mallory knew more than all of them—she was sure of it.

It didn't take too long to locate Burns in the kitchen, drinking a cup of coffee himself, although it took a little longer to make him understand that she needed his employer's medication. It was the elderly plump cook who responded the quickest, producing a bottle of pills.

Brianna hurried back to the library. Giles was still sitting exactly as she had left him, and the tablet she gave him seemed to work almost instantly, colour slowly returning to his cheeks, although he still looked haggard.

Brianna frowned. 'I think you need to rest for a while—'

'I've been resting for twenty-one years,' he stated tersely, although he put his head back in the chair and wearily closed his eyes.

Since Brianna was born. Since Rebecca had died...

He drew in a ragged breath before opening his eyes to look up at Brianna. 'I think I will rest for a short time,' he conceded. 'But then I want to talk to you again. Alone this time. Come back at four o'clock,' he instructed autocratically.

She could see that Nathan was alarmed at this suggestion, but, having now met Giles Mallory, she didn't think she had anything to fear from him. He was rude, bad-tempered, incredibly bossy, but she could handle all of that.

'I'll come back at four,' she agreed.

'I don't think that's a good idea at all,' Nathan told her abruptly on the walk back to the Landris house, his dark scowl evidence of his displeasure.

'I need to talk to him,' she persisted. 'And I think he might be more open with me if I'm on my own.' She almost had to run to keep pace with Nathan's long, forceful strides.

He glared at her. 'I don't want you to be hurt by anything he has to say.'

'I don't think Giles wants to hurt me,' she said carefully. 'That wasn't the impression he gave me at all.' In fact, the more she thought of their visit the more convinced she was that Giles Mallory was actually pleased she had gone to see him.

'What he has to tell you may hurt you,' Nathan insisted.

She shook her head. 'Not if it's the truth.'

'And what makes you think it will be?' Nathan turned on her angrily, after coming to an abrupt halt. 'He can say what he damn well pleases, because there's no one to dispute what he says!'

Brianna faced Nathan unflinchingly. 'I think he will tell me the truth.'

'And just exactly how do I explain your absence when you disappear this afternoon?' Nathan challenged.

Her mouth twisted thoughtfully. 'Tell them we've had an argument and I've gone off for a walk on my own. The way this conversation's going, it won't be far from the truth, anyway!' she sighed.

'I'm only trying to protect you.'

'And I appreciate it.'

'No, you don't, damn it!' Nathan was furious now, that cool reserve completely gone. 'You're headstrong, determined, irresponsible—'

'I am not!' she returned as furiously, and the two of them stood glaring at each other in the middle of the wood that separated the Landris and Mallory houses. 'I have never been irresponsible in my life!'

'Well, you're being so now,' Nathan accused. 'I never wanted you to see Giles in the first place, let alone—'

'Why was that, Nathan?' She looked at him with defiant eyes.

'I just told you—'

'It was to protect me,' she finished. 'Well, I've met him now, Nathan—and, to be honest, I can't see much there that I need protecting from! Admittedly, he's sharp to the point of rudeness, but other than that—'

'He hasn't even started yet, Brianna,' Nathan insisted. 'And yet you insist on going back there this afternoon on your own—now if that isn't irresponsible, then I don't know what is!'

There were two bright spots of angry colour in her cheeks. 'That isn't being irresponsible, Nathan—it's my right! I'm grateful to you for all the help you've given me over this last week, but now I—'

'Don't need me any more!' he interrupted savagely, tightly grasping the tops of her arms.

'I didn't say that!' she gasped—at the tightness of his grasp as much as anything else.

'You didn't need to,' he exclaimed. 'You've made it more than obvious that I've just been a means to an end.'

'That isn't true,' she protested incredulously. 'I—I like you.' She understated her emotions where he was concerned, completely shaken by his vehemence.

His eyes darkened before his head lowered and his mouth came down forcefully on hers, his arms moving tightly about her waist as he moulded her body against his, his lips moving against hers, fiercely demanding.

It was like none of the other kisses they had shared, and Nathan's lack of gentleness instantly made Brianna want to pull away. And then she was caught up in the passion, returning the kiss, her arms moving up about his shoulders, loving the hard, muscular strength of him.

The mossy grass was soft against her back as Nathan lowered her down onto it, their mouths still fused together as the lean length of him half lay across her, telling of a pulsing desire that was way out of control!

Nathan pushed her jumper up out of the way, revealing the pale blue lacy bra she wore, his lips warm and caressing against the creamy skin he had exposed.

But it wasn't enough. Brianna wanted more, reaching up herself to release the front fastening to her bra, her back arching in ecstasy as Nathan's mouth moved to possessively claim the rosy tip of her breast, his tongue moving moistly against that hardened nub, one of his hands cupping the softness of her other breast.

Brianna was filled with heat, burning, a need that surged through every particle of her body. One of her hands cradled Nathan's head as he suckled moistly, then she felt the air cold against the moistness as he turned his attention to her other breast.

She moved restlessly against him, caught up in the pleasure even as she knew she wanted more, so much more...

But, as if becoming aware of that need, and the complete unsuitability of their surroundings for taking it further, Nathan moved suddenly away from her, rolling over onto his back, one arm thrown over his eyes as he breathed rapidly.

Brianna was dazed by his sudden desertion, turning to look at him as he lay beside her, her face paling slightly as she found he had moved his arm and was now looking at her too. And what she saw in his eyes made her scramble to her feet, quickly fastening her bra as she did so, before straightening her jumper. Nathan looked horrified at the intimacy they had just shared.

She couldn't even look at him again as he got to his feet beside her, her gaze stopping somewhere in the middle of his chest. 'We should be getting back for lunch,' she said thickly.

'Brianna—'

'Forget it, Nathan,' she dismissed jerkily. 'Emotions are running a little high at the moment, and—'

'Damn the excuses!' He grasped her arms once again. 'I kissed you because I wanted to.'

'And I took things a step further.' She shook her head at her own lack of inhibition with this man. Only with this man...

He released one of her arms, his hand moving to

wrench her chin up, forcing her gaze to meet his stormy one. 'I wanted it to go a lot further than that,' he rasped harshly. 'It's just— I—'

'I understand, Nathan.' She brushed aside his hesitation.

'No, damn it, you don't,' he bit out forcefully. 'This isn't the right time, Brianna. Or the right place either.' He looked around at the surrounding trees and undergrowth.

He was right about that, she knew he was, and yet she also knew there was more to it than that. And she couldn't help remembering her response, that complete lack of inhibition. She had almost thrown herself at him!

'Lunch,' she reminded him in an overbright voice.

'Brianna, we need to talk—'

'When it's the right time and the right place.' She put her arm through the crook of his. 'We really should be getting back now—before your family sends out a search party!'

He looked as if he would like to protest further, but Brianna returned his gaze with steady determination.

They didn't talk on the rest of their walk back to the Landris home, and Brianna was relieved, rather than disappointed, that she wasn't seated next to him during lunch either. Sam was once again on her left, with Peter Landris, at the head of the table, on her other side. She was glad of the younger woman's presence, letting Sam chatter on but adding little to the conversation herself, very aware of Nathan seated next to his mother at the other end of the table, but deliberately keeping her eyes averted.

'Have you and my dear cousin argued?' Sam whispered when they reached the coffee stage of the meal.

Brianna met her question frowningly. 'Sorry?'

Sam grinned unabashedly. 'You're completely ignoring Nathan at the other end of the table, and he keeps giving you worried glances when he thinks no one else is looking; I thought perhaps the two of you had argued?'

Brianna bit her lip. 'Does anyone ever argue with Nathan?' And win!

'I do,' Sam answered brightly. 'But then I always have.' She shrugged. 'I know he can be a little stuffy at times, but—'

'We haven't argued, Sam,' Brianna cut in softly. 'I think perhaps Nathan sees me—a little differently, here amongst his own family.' She excused the coolness between them.

The other woman looked puzzled. 'I don't know what you mean…?'

Brianna sighed. 'I'm a doctor's daughter, Sam. I work as a hospital receptionist.'

'I hope you aren't saying what I think you are,' Sam replied. 'Because that is the biggest load of nonsense I've ever heard. This is just a family, like any other—'

'I don't think so,' Brianna chided teasingly. They were seated at a dining-table laid with crystal glassware and silver cutlery, being waited on by servants, the meal itself having been cooked by yet another employee in the kitchen at the back of the house.

'Nathan is not a snob,' Sam defended, indignant on his behalf. 'None of us are really. I know I made those remarks about Aunt Margaret yesterday, but actually she's okay too.' She glanced across at Margaret Landris as she chatted to her sister Clarissa. 'They can be very kind,' Sam added with feeling.

Brianna shook her head. 'I don't have a problem with your family, Sam—'

'They're Nathan's family, too,' the other woman reminded her sharply. 'Good grief, Nathan's fiancée was a secretary—he met her in the courts!'

'The engagement didn't work out,' Brianna observed.

'Not because the family didn't approve of who she was and what she did,' Sam came back swiftly. 'Sarah was a gold-digger. And luckily Nathan discovered that before the two of them were married.'

It pained Brianna to think of Nathan being wanted for any other reason than himself; his obvious wealth was more of a stumbling block to their relationship than an incentive! 'Once bitten, twice shy,' she muttered.

'You aren't a gold-digger,' Sam denied unreservedly.

'No, I'm not,' Brianna agreed; this conversation had become altogether too serious.

'Anyone can see that—even Margaret.' Sam grimaced. 'All of this—' she indicated their surroundings '—puts you off rather than encouraging you to want to be part of it. Now, I could believe you and Nathan have argued about that!'

'I told you, we haven't argued,' Brianna persisted. 'I think we're—things have perhaps moved too quickly. For both of us.' She paused. She certainly hadn't wanted to fall in love with Nathan. At any time, let alone now!

'I'm not sure I can believe that either,' Sam said. 'Nathan has never been a person who does things on impulse—in fact the opposite,' she reflected affectionately.

That might be so, but Brianna very much doubted what had happened between them in the woods this morning had been planned; Nathan had seemed as disturbed by the intensity of emotion between them as she had been!

She laughed lightly. 'Stop looking so worried, Sam, Nathan and I are fine.'

His cousin didn't look convinced. 'I just wouldn't like to see him hurt again...'

Brianna squeezed her arm. 'I have no intention of hurting him.' But she couldn't say the same about herself; loving Nathan was pure madness!

And he seemed to consider her going to see Giles again alone was equal madness; the two of them argued about that once more later in the afternoon, before Brianna set off for the Mallory home. Nathan was adamant she was going to be hurt, and Brianna was equally as determined she was going anyway. The two of them parted angrily, Brianna still smarting when she was shown into the library where Rebecca's father waited for her.

Giles studied her through narrowed lids. 'Nathan didn't approve of your coming here alone,' he guessed.

Brianna gave him an angry glance. 'You knew he wouldn't,' she said flatly, as she sat down uninvited in one of the armchairs that flanked the fireplace.

'He cares for you,' Giles shrugged.

'Or maybe he just knows you better than I do,' she returned, unwilling to discuss Nathan with this man.

Giles sat forward in his chair, looking much better than he had earlier, the colour back in his cheeks, that glitter of challenge in his eyes. 'Do you want to know me better, Brianna?' he asked.

She swallowed hard. 'I—want to know what happened all those years ago.'

He nodded. 'And you think I can tell you.'

'I know you can,' she responded firmly.

Giles relaxed back in his chair. 'Not all of it, girl. I don't know all of it. But I can tell you what I do know,' he added as she would have protested. 'So just sit there and hold your tongue until I've finished. Do you think you can do that?'

Her mouth twisted wryly. 'You obviously don't think I can!'

'No.' He sighed heavily. 'It's amazing, Brianna, you were brought up completely different from Rebecca, in a totally different family, you never even knew your real mother, and yet you're so like her. And not just to look at. Looking at you now, hearing you speak, it's like going back over twenty years and talking to her. I'm glad you decided to come here, Brianna. Don't look so worried, girl. I'm not about to go all sentimental on you. I'm too old for that. I accepted long ago that I've lived my life, and none of it can be changed, especially the mistakes. The people who can forgive me for those are already dead, so I just have to go on living with them!'

'Tell me,' Brianna encouraged.

'Where to begin...?' He leant his head back against the chair, closing his eyes. 'Probably with the gauche farmer's son who fell in love with the daughter of the man who actually owned the land his own father farmed. That's me, by the way, Brianna,' he told her with self-mockery.

She had already guessed that, but she said nothing, determined to just sit and listen to him.

'Joanne was beautiful. Blonde, blue-eyed—and, at nineteen, ten years younger than me. The family lived here during the summer months, and I loved Joanne for years before she ever really noticed me. That was why I had never married before, much to my own family's chagrin. And then one summer things seemed to change,' he went on warmly. 'Joanne had been away for a year, at some finishing school or other, and when she came here for the summer we began to go out riding together. How I loved those times, loved just being with Joanne. She seemed to feel the same way, which finally gave me the courage to ask her to marry me.'

The love he had felt was still there in his voice, and Brianna felt the prick of tears in her eyes as she continued to listen to him.

'I was amazed when she said yes, and unsurprised when her family objected—quite happy for us to run off together and get married when Joanne said it was the only thing for us to do. I know, shades of Rebecca,' Giles acknowledged at Brianna's knowing look. 'But I'll get to Rebecca in a moment...' He paused. 'Joanne's family were furious at the marriage, but her parents finally relented enough to give us this house. Joanne was accepted back as their daughter, but I was never approved of, never forgiven for stealing her away from them. As you can guess, everyone predicted the marriage wouldn't last, which just made me all the more determined to prove them wrong.' He gave a rueful shake of his head at the memory.

It was almost possible to visualise the young man he must have been, to feel the delight he had felt to at last be married to the woman he loved.

'And then I realised that Joanne had married me on the rebound,' he added heavily. 'That she had been so reckless and defiant during that summer we fell in love because of a love affair with another man that had gone wrong—because the man was about to marry someone else.'

Brianna stared at him. And then history had repeated itself twenty years later... The circumstances hadn't been quite the same, but enough to be called an incredible coincidence!

Giles met her gaze steadily. 'I didn't realise it for some time, but the penny did finally drop—once Joanne's parents gave us this house and we were actually living next door to the man!'

Brianna gazed open-eyed across at him. Next door...?

But Peter and Margaret Landris lived next door! Peter Landris…?

Giles noticed her horrified expression. 'Now you understand why I didn't want Nathan here this afternoon.'

She swallowed hard. This couldn't be; it just couldn't. And then she again remembered Peter Landris's bitterness over the way Joanne's marriage to Giles had turned out, the way he had stared at her because she was so like Rebecca. Or so like Joanne…?

Giles drew in a ragged breath. 'I became consumed with jealousy, even though Joanne assured me the affair had been over before she married me, that it was me she loved and not Peter. I couldn't believe her, couldn't see how she could possibly love someone as unpolished as me after someone like Peter Landris.

'I became obsessed with keeping Joanne to myself—it's the only way I can think of to describe the madness that took me over! If we were always together, then there was no chance of her ever being with anyone else. Even when she became pregnant, gave birth to our daughter, I couldn't stand even that pull on her love.' His face contorted with pain as he remembered his obsession. 'Do you believe me when I say I'm telling you the truth, girl?' he rasped harshly at Brianna as she sat in silence.

Oh, yes, she believed him. How could she not? He was sparing himself nothing, not even that mindless obsession that had ultimately only destroyed himself, as well as those he loved.

She nodded, an ache in her heart for this man who had loved too deeply.

'Rebecca grew up hating me,' he continued flatly. 'That isn't surprising. I took her mother away from her. Joanne and I travelled, stayed away for months at a time.

And even when we were home I had little time for Rebecca, was content only if I had Joanne to myself. It must have been torturous for Joanne, trying to balance our marriage and the love she felt for our daughter. And then Joanne died.' His voice shook emotionally as he inwardly relived the death of the wife he had simply loved too much. 'And the obsession ended with her.'

As obsessions usually did... How tragic. What a waste. What absolute hell—

'I was left,' Giles said, evenly, 'with a life that no longer had any light or happiness in it. And a daughter of thirteen I didn't even know—and who hated me with a vengeance! You don't have to tell me it could all have been so different, Brianna,' he cried as he saw the anguish in her face. 'I've had years to realise that. Years and years. Because, believe it or not, despite what other people may have told you, Joanne did love me. She would never have put up with the way I was if she hadn't loved me.'

His face softened at the memory of his wife. 'She tried for so many years to convince me of that. I just didn't—I couldn't accept—' He drew in a harshly controlling breath. 'Rebecca refused to have anything to do with me after her mother died, would only come back here if she knew I wouldn't be at home. I made sure I was away a lot. I owed her that much. I had left it too late to give her anything else—she wouldn't accept anything.' He bowed his head. 'I made my marriage a living hell because I loved Joanne so much, and in the end I lost her, anyway. And our daughter could never forgive me for the years when I hadn't wanted her.'

It was all exactly as Nathan and his father had told her, the only missing factor being this man's obsessive love for Joanne. A love that had become an obsession because of Joanne's previous relationship with Peter

Landris...! Without that information it had all sounded so cold and calculated, cruel even. The knowledge of Giles Mallory's love, the reason he'd become so obsessive, didn't make any of it less tragic, but it did explain so many of his actions.

'I did try to get through to Rebecca,' Giles continued with a croak in his voice. 'She made it clear I had left it too late. By about thirteen years.' He groaned with self-recrimination. 'We barely spoke for the next five. The last conversation we had together was when she told me she was pregnant.' He stopped speaking briefly, and then went on, 'She said that the affair was over. That the baby's father was none of my business. The relationship was over, but she intended having the baby.'

'The baby you wanted her to abort.' Brianna couldn't keep silent on this—she was that baby!

'No,' Giles barked loudly, firmly shaking his head. 'I saw that baby as a possible way for Rebecca and I to finally find a way back to a father and daughter relationship. I wanted to take care of them both.'

'But she ran away—'

'Not from me!' His voice rose angrily. 'I don't expect you to believe that. Why should you? No one else did,' he added bitterly. 'Everyone assumed I had thrown my pregnant daughter out of the house, that I had disowned her. When in fact it was the complete opposite. I saw Rebecca's pregnancy as a chance for us to finally get to know each other.'

He turned away from Brianna, staring sightlessly from his chair at the clock that stood on the mantelpiece. 'Rebecca told me before she left that she didn't want to bring her child up here. That she would rather give her baby away to strangers than let me have anything to do with my grandchild's future.'

The words of an angry young woman who had suffered through a painful childhood... Rebecca had felt it was too late, even for forgiveness.

Giles turned back to Brianna, a flame burning deep in his eyes. 'Which is exactly what she did,' he grated. 'And two days after giving you away she deliberately took her own life!'

Brianna chewed hard on her bottom lip. A family pulled apart by a love that was so possessively strong it had destroyed rather than built. 'You didn't go to her funeral.' She couldn't soften towards this man, not completely. He had caused so much unhappiness, no matter what the reason.

He closed his eyes again, swallowing hard. 'I did what I thought Rebecca would have wanted—probably for the first time in her life,' he acknowledged with self-disgust. 'I had let her down so many times when she was alive, I refused to do it when she was dead.'

'And her baby?' Brianna prompted chokily. 'Your own grandchild?'

'A grandchild I had no right to,' he bit out fiercely. 'Rebecca had made it very plain to me that she didn't want me in her child's life, so once again I acceded to her wishes. She had placed you with people she trusted would love you—'

'They have,' Brianna confirmed softly.

'I know that,' Giles gritted. 'I may not have been part of your life, Brianna, but I knew where you were, that you were happy.'

She had ceased to be surprised at the amount of people who knew so much about her life, one she had lived in absolute ignorance of their interest. 'And my real father?' she insisted tensely.

'I can't help you there, Brianna,' he admitted. 'All I know is that your mother loved him, that he's the reason she left here over twenty-one years ago. She refused to tell me who he was, said her involvement with him had caused too much pain already, without any more damage being done.'

Another cul-de-sac.

Did no one know who her biological father was?

Only the man himself, it seemed—and if he hadn't been willing to reveal himself all those years ago, when Rebecca had needed him so much, then he wasn't going to do so now!

CHAPTER EIGHT

'YOU know, don't you, Brianna?'

She looked up at Peter Landris as he stood further down the hallway. She had only just returned to the Landris home after leaving Giles Mallory, and she was still feeling extremely fragile after her harrowing conversation with the elderly man who was her grandfather. The things he had told her were heartbreaking, and she knew it would help to ease some of his pain if he felt she at least forgave him. But she wasn't ready to do that yet...

And she wasn't quite sure of Nathan's father any more...

She met his gaze warily. 'I know what?' She was deliberately vague.

He gave a half-smile, opening the door behind him. 'Come into my study for a few minutes, Brianna,' he invited gruffly.

She hesitated only briefly before preceding him into the elegantly furnished room. She knew so much more now than when she had last spoken to him—and none of it was good!

'Nathan told me you had gone over to talk to Giles,' Peter Landris told her, as he indicted she should sit down in one of the comfortable armchairs, before sitting in another himself. 'Giles will have told you about my relationship with Joanne,' he stated frankly.

Brianna met his eyes challengingly. 'And you want to know whether or not I intend telling Nathan,' she guessed.

He shook his head. 'Not really.' He gave a sad smile. 'It was forty years ago, Brianna,' he explained at her sceptical expression. 'I wasn't even married to Nathan's mother at the time.'

'But—'

'We were engaged, but not married,' he explained at Brianna's frowning expression. 'I have been married to Margaret for forty years and I have never been unfaithful to her. Joanne and I shared a couple of weeks of madness in Switzerland, when she was away at finishing school there and I was travelling on business. I'm not going to make any excuses for my behaviour—I was engaged to be married and shouldn't have been in a relationship with another woman—but Joanne was... Never mind,' he dismissed raggedly. 'It shouldn't have happened, and I returned home to marry Margaret after that two weeks with Joanne. A few months later your grandmother married Giles.'

'On the rebound, surely?' Brianna half accused, not willing to let this man off so lightly. Although she had to admit she agreed with Giles; Joanne would never have put up with his behaviour as a husband if she hadn't been genuinely in love with him.

'I don't think so.' Peter Landris shook his head. 'For a while I did think that might be the case. Until Joanne assured me otherwise. Oh, yes, Brianna, we stayed friends,' he said, meeting her surprised expression. 'She insisted she was in love with her husband, hoped that in time he might actually come to believe it himself. I may not have liked the way their marriage was, but Joanne was totally loyal to Giles. It wasn't until Joanne was dead that Giles and I actually talked about that situation, and by then it was too late—' He broke off as Nathan burst in unannounced. 'It's customary to knock before entering an occupied room,' his father reproved caustically.

Nathan looked unperturbed by the reprimand; his worried gaze was fixed on Brianna. 'Are you all right?' he asked urgently.

She glanced at Peter Landris, unsure whether he had ever told his wife of his relationship with Joanne but absolutely positive Nathan didn't know about it. 'I'm fine.' She turned back to Nathan, her tone reassuring. 'As I was just telling your father, Giles was absolutely no help in identifying Rebecca's lover.'

She stood up, carefully avoiding Peter Landris's eyes. 'I think I would like to go up to my room now and freshen up. I expect we'll be leaving soon, Nathan?' she added pointedly, anxious to get away from here now. She had so much information to think about and she needed to be able to do it alone, in the comfort of her own home.

Nathan looked across at her, obviously not in the least reassured by her casual dismissal of her meeting with Giles. 'Whenever you're ready,' he responded distractedly.

'I'll freshen up and get my things,' she agreed readily.

'You still need to come into the office to discuss your inheritance,' Peter Landris reminded her as she reached the door.

And finish their conversation, she guessed...

She shook her head. 'The more I hear about what money did for my mother, and grandmother, the less I want anything to do with it.' She was sure that if Giles hadn't married a woman with money he wouldn't have been as insecure in his love, and, if he hadn't been so, maybe they would have been a normal family. Maybe... She did know that she had survived very well so far without money—happily so.

'I can understand that you feel that way now,' Peter Landris sympathised. 'But when you're ready, do come in to see me.'

Having to go to the offices of Landris, Landris and Davis was another reason why, for the moment at least, she didn't want anything to do with Rebecca's will. 'I'll let you know,' she answered vaguely. 'And thank you for your hospitality this weekend. I realise it hasn't been an easy situation for you, and I do appreciate that.' She met the older man's gaze squarely, trying silently to let him know that, as far as she was concerned, his relationship with Joanne was the past, and, as such, it should remain there.

After all, she did have the answers to some of her questions. She was left with a few new queries she hadn't even anticipated, but for the main part it had been a successful visit.

'Do you intend seeing Giles again?' Peter Landris prompted gently.

Before coming here she had disliked the old man intensely; as he had so easily guessed himself, she had considered him a tyrannical despot. But now… He was just a lonely old man, with nothing left in his life but the memories of a past that had to cause him as much pain as they did happiness.

'I don't know,' she answered truthfully.

Giles had asked her the same thing when she'd left him a short time ago, and she hadn't known what the answer to the question was then, either. She needed time—and space—to think about that.

'Will you go back to see Giles?' Nathan glanced at her as he drove them both back into town.

She hesitated. 'I don't know,' she answered again honestly.

Nathan had turned his attention back to the road ahead. 'It was a difficult meeting for you,' he observed grimly.

It had been difficult—but not half as difficult as realising she was in love with this man seated beside her!

'It was emotionally tough.' She leant her head back against the car seat. 'But it's hard to continue hating someone who already hates himself so much.'

And Giles did hate himself, for the marriage he had smothered, for losing the daughter he had left it far too late to love. Although Brianna did accept he hadn't compounded those mistakes by claiming his grandchild all those years ago, even though he had known exactly where she was. That meant he couldn't be all bad...

'He does, doesn't he?' Nathan acknowledged quietly. 'I never realised that myself until today...'

'Don't start to feel sorry for him, Nathan. Giles wouldn't thank you for it!'

'How right you are!' he agreed.

They lapsed into silence for the rest of the journey, Brianna aware, with each mile that passed, that they would soon be parting. Probably for ever. There was simply no reason for them to ever meet again.

Her heart sank altogether as Nathan parked the car outside her home, and it took all her effort to force a smile to her lips as she turned to him. 'Thank you for your help this weekend, Nathan—'

'Don't try and dismiss me in the same way you did my father earlier.' He turned to her, his eyes glittering. 'This morning may not have been the right time or the right place, but the next time will be!' He tightly held her upper arms. 'I'm going to call you in a couple of days and invite you out to dinner.'

Brianna blinked up at him, thoughts racing erratically

through her mind. She wasn't sure it was a good idea for Nathan to invite her anywhere!

'And you—' he shook her slightly '—are going to accept!'

'I am?' she returned shortly.

'You are,' he told her arrogantly. 'I want to get to know you better, Brianna—not in that way!' he proved as she raised sceptical brows. 'We met in the first place through strange circumstances, and—perhaps emotions have been running a little high because of that.'

'You've been talking to Sam,' she realised knowingly.

'She's been talking to me,' he corrected self-derisively. 'I don't know if you've realised it yet, but Sam actually rarely listens to anything anyone else has to say!'

Sam had obviously listened during her conversation with Brianna earlier—and had felt strongly enough about what had been said to talk to Nathan about it while Brianna was out this afternoon!

'There is absolutely no reason for you to invite me out to dinner, Nathan—'

'Of course there's a reason, damn it! Haven't I just explained I want to see you again?'

Not exactly. Although perhaps in his own way he had...

'I'm not sure it's wise for us to see each other again, Nathan,' she answered slowly. In view of the way his family seemed to be so entangled in her past, she wasn't sure of that at all!

He released her, sitting back. 'Has someone else come into your life?' His eyes narrowed ominously. 'Perhaps the doctor I saw you talking to the other day?'

He meant Jim. And although they might have been a little more than just friends for a while, that was all they were now.

'My hesitation has nothing to do with anyone in or out of my life. I—I think I need time, to adjust to all that's happened this last week.' If she ever did; it seemed so incredible, it was hard to believe!

'That's why I suggested leaving it a couple of days,' Nathan said carefully. 'Or is it that you don't want to see me again?'

'Now that you've outlived your usefulness as a means to an end?' she returned, using his own words.

Irritation flickered across the hardness of his features. 'I was angry when I said that—'

'You're angry now, too,' she pointed out gently.

'You seem to make me that way!' he grated. 'You're self-willed, opinionated, totally infuriating—' He broke off as she began to laugh softly. 'What is so funny?' He scowled darkly.

Her laughter faded, but she still smiled. 'I'm all those things—and more!' she reminded him. 'And yet you still want to see me again?'

He couldn't hold back his own smile. 'Because you're also open, funny, honest—and very beautiful,' he told her.

Brianna sobered, reaching out to gently touch the hardness of his cheek. 'I'm just not sure an "us" is a good idea. We still don't know who I really am.' She gave a pained grimace. She had always thought she knew exactly who she was, and what she wanted, but this last week had thrown her whole life into confusion.

Part of her wished so badly that she had never received that letter from Peter Landris. She had been happy just being Brianna Gibson, beloved daughter of Graham and Jean Gibson. Knowing she was the grand-daughter of Joanne and Giles Mallory, the daughter of Rebecca Mallory and an unnamed man, had thrown her into emotional chaos. But at the same time she knew that if she had never learnt all those things, she would never have met Nathan either...

Nathan took her hand. 'I didn't expect you to come along with a signed and sealed pedigree!' he protested.

'You *did*,' she insisted. 'And the truth is, I could be anyone's daughter. Anyone's at all...'

He frowned at the shadows in her eyes. 'Are we back to my uncle James again?'

'Not necessarily,' she answered. 'Although I still don't think he can be ruled out. Nathan, it would be awful if we—came to care about each other and then found out we're cousins!' she groaned. It wouldn't be just awful, it would be disastrous!'

'That's purely a supposition on your part—'

'You're starting to sound like a lawyer again, Nathan,' she teased.

'I am a lawyer!' He frowned darkly. 'And until someone can prove otherwise, I choose to believe we are unrelated.'

'But—'

'*Can* you prove otherwise?' Nathan prompted harshly. 'Did Giles tell you *anything* this afternoon that suggested we could be related?'

No, he hadn't done that, but he had told her of the relationship Nathan's father had with Joanne...

She turned away, unable to meet his probing gaze. 'No,' she answered flatly. 'I just wouldn't like us to become—close and then discover a relationship between us is impossible.' Her eyes were a deep, troubled blue.

He pulled her into his arms. 'We're already close, Brianna,' he murmured, his breath stirring the hair at her temple. 'Didn't this morning prove that?'

She gave a shaky smile, eyes misted with tears. 'You're big on proof, aren't you, Nathan?' she attempted to tease.

'Circumstantial evidence is exactly that,' he said seriously. 'And that's all you have so far. It's all you may ever have. And I'm not about to shut the door on an "us" because of something so flimsy. I will call you, Brianna,' he repeated firmly, gently kissing her on the lips. 'And you will come out to dinner with me,' he added sternly.

'I will,' she acquiesced huskily, unable to deny him anything when he held her close against him like this.

'She finally agrees!' He raised his eyes heavenwards. 'Ten minutes of argument and you give me the answer I wanted in the first place.' He shook his head. 'It's going to wear me out if we have to do this every time I ask you out.'

'You won't have to,' she assured him. He was right, all she had so far was circumstantial evidence—and the fact that she loved him! At this moment in time, the latter felt much more important than the former...!

'Thank God for that!' He kissed her hard before moving away. 'I'll see you in a few days, Brianna.'

She got out of the car, taking her overnight bag with her, hurrying up the pathway to unlock the front door so she could go inside. She didn't so much as glance back at Nathan. Because she didn't dare. Half of her wanted to run back into his arms, to feel the protection of his embrace. And the other half of her knew she couldn't, because, despite her agreement to see him again, she still wasn't sure being with him again was a good idea...!

Her father sat in the lounge, glancing up from some papers he had been studying. 'Did you have a good weekend?' he enquired, getting up as she entered the room.

He looked so vulnerable standing there, his expression so wary, as if prepared to ward off a blow. All of this must be so awful for him too, Brianna knew.

'Oh, Daddy!' She flung herself into the arms of the only man she ever wanted to know as her father, sobbing out the sadness of meeting Giles, the unanswered questions.

The only part she left out was her newly discovered feelings for Nathan...

'You're looking thin, Brianna.' Nathan looked assessingly across the dinner table at her.

He had waited, as he had said he would, until Wednesday morning before telephoning her and inviting her out to dinner that evening.

Brianna had wanted to refuse him, had see-sawed the previous two days between wanting to see him again and knowing it wasn't a good idea that she did. But when he had actually telephoned this morning she hadn't been able to say no...

And he was right; she had lost a couple of pounds. All of this was proving just too much for her, and she had lived on nervous energy since the weekend, couldn't seem to settle to anything for longer than two minutes, and the very thought of food made her feel ill. If this was love, she was never going to survive it!

She gave him an overbright smile. 'Have you never heard the saying "you can never be too thin or too rich"? One out of two isn't bad!'

Nathan didn't return her smile, his gaze reproving on the dark shadows beneath her eyes and the hollows in her cheeks. 'We both know that isn't true,' he said. 'You're too thin. And money never brought anyone real happiness.'

He wasn't making this easy for her. She didn't want to be serious this evening; she wanted to be that carefree woman she had been ten days ago—before she knew anything of her other family.

'Not for the want of trying,' she responded breezily, before taking a sip of the wine he had ordered to accompany their meal.

'Talking of money—'

'Which we weren't!' she cut in sharply, knowing exactly what he was going to say—and she didn't want to hear it. 'At least, only in the abstract,' she conceded. 'This is a nice restaurant, Nathan.' She looked about them admiringly, at the tastefully upmarket surroundings. Not the same restaurant he had taken her to last week, but one that was just as exclusive. 'I've never been here before.' Which wasn't surprising, either— there weren't even any prices listed on the menu, so she could only guess at its exclusivity! Nathan must have booked this table several days ago, because the restaurant was full.

'Brianna, I accept that the subject is painful to you, but my father wanted me to tell you—'

'Let him tell me,' she interrupted. 'When I'm ready to hear it! Are you saying he knows the two of us have come out to dinner this evening?' She very much doubted Peter Landris approved of her continuing to see his son.

'Only in the abstract.' Nathan repeated her earlier comment. 'He overheard me on the telephone at the office booking a table for this evening, and he guessed who I was having dinner with.'

She tensed. 'And?'

Nathan's mouth tightened. 'And nothing. Brianna, I stopped asking for my parents' approval of my movements fifteen years ago!'

'And your friends?'

'Them too,' he confirmed abruptly.

She sighed. 'Nathan—'

'Brianna!' One of his hands moved possessively to

cover the nervous movements of hers on the table-top, his gaze searching on the paleness of her face. 'Let's get out of here,' he suggested, signalling the waiter and asking for their bill.

To the waiter's credit, he didn't even blink an eyelid at the fact that they weren't staying to eat the meal they had ordered!

'Where are we going?' Brianna was breathless with the speed with which Nathan had paid their bill and hurried her out of the restaurant. 'Nathan, you know what those people in there are thinking!' she protested, as he stopped guiding her along the pavement and unlocked the car door for her to get inside.

In fact, the restaurant staff had all behaved with absolute discretion as the bill was paid, Brianna's jacket was brought back to her and the restaurant door opened for their departure, but the speculation in their eyes had been unmistakable!

'That I can't even wait to feed you before making love to you,' Nathan joked as he climbed into the car beside her. 'They were right.' He turned on the ignition. 'I can't!'

'But— I—'

'Speechless at last,' he announced with grim satisfaction, driving with his usual precise ease. 'And, to answer your initial question, we're going to my home.'

Brianna stared at him in the semi-darkness. 'I— What happened to wanting to get to know me?' she gasped. 'The right place and the right time?'

He barely glanced at her. 'My home is the right place, and I can't think of a better time,' he replied.

She remembered the little he had told her about his home in London, how it was nothing like the show-place that was his parents' home. Her interest had been piqued then. But if she had ever thought she would see where

Nathan lived, she had never thought it would be in these circumstances.

'Nathan, I don't think you can be thinking straight—'

'I haven't done that since the moment I met you!' he confessed. 'You're constantly on my mind, Brianna. I can't even concentrate on my work.'

For a man whose work seemed to have been his whole life during the last five years, since the end of his engagement, that was quite an admission.

Maybe it wouldn't hurt for her to go to his home, just for a short time...

Nathan drove her to a tall Victorian house in the suburbs of London, an obviously affluent neighbourhood from the look of the surrounding property and the expensive cars parked in the driveways. But the inside of Nathan's house was exactly what he had said it was: a home rather than a show-piece. The colour scheme was in muted golds and greens and the furniture comfortable; there was also a general air of untidyness about the place, as if the years of restraint during his childhood had finally burst forth.

'Well?' Nathan was watching her reaction intently as she looked around the sitting-room.

He looked unsure of himself—not an emotion Brianna had ever associated with him before!—as if her opinion really mattered to him.

She smiled. 'It's a lovely house, Nathan,' she told him unreservedly. 'You must love coming home here in the evenings.'

'I do.' He seemed relieved by her approval, moving to a drinks cabinet at the side of the room, opening the mini-bar beneath it and taking out a bottle of chilled white wine. 'Shall we make some food to go with this?' He held up the as yet unopened bottle. 'I'm sure we'll be able to find something in the fridge. And I have deprived you of your meal.'

He wasn't completely to blame for their early departure; if she was honest, she had wanted to leave too. They couldn't really have talked at the restaurant. And they couldn't have behaved like polite strangers either. They were well past that!

But, at the same time, she wasn't sure the two of them being alone here was a good idea, either. It was far, far too private. Too intimate. But getting dinner together, and sitting down to eat it, meant she could be in Nathan's company a while longer...

'Brianna?' he persisted. 'I feel as if I'm in a courtroom, awaiting the verdict!'

God, how she loved this man!

She smiled at him again, her eyes glowing. 'The verdict is yes!' she told him laughingly.

She followed him through to the kitchen, enjoying just watching him move, the way the darkness of his hair brushed against his collar, the wide strength of his shoulders, the tall maleness of him. *He* had been constantly on *her* mind the last three days, too!

Letting him go out of her life was going to be the hardest thing she had ever done in her life!

But she didn't believe it was an option—it was a necessity...

They made omelettes, accompanied by crusty bread and salad, liberally imbibing the wine Nathan had opened as they prepared the meal together. By the time they sat down to eat in the huge old-fashioned kitchen, Brianna felt slightly light-headed.

So much so that she couldn't even have said what they talked about as they ate, although she knew they laughed a lot together.

'I enjoyed that,' Nathan murmured as they stood up a short time later to clear away.

'We were hungry,' she agreed, wondering if Nathan, like her, hadn't been eating properly the last couple of days; he had certainly seemed hungry enough just now.

'I wasn't talking about the food. Oh, I enjoyed that—' he acknowledged his empty plate '—but I enjoyed the preparation too. It was fun doing it together.'

It *had* been fun. But Brianna was also now more convinced than ever that coming here had not been a good idea. They were just too alone!

'Nathan, I have to go now,' she told him quietly, now that everything was tidied away. 'I've enjoyed seeing your home. The meal was excellent—'

'What about the company?' he rasped huskily, his gaze intense.

Brianna avoided meeting it. 'I enjoyed the company too,' she said slowly.

'But now you have to go.'

'Yes,' she said forcefully, her eyes flashing deeply blue as she looked up at him. 'Now I have to go.'

His jaw was set, a nerve pulsing in his cheek. 'I don't want you to.'

She didn't really want to go. Not now. Not ever. But one of them had to be sensible about this. And it didn't seem as if it was going to be Nathan!

'Maybe when all of this is over—'

'It is over, Brianna.' He moved forward to put his arms about her and pull her close against the hard strength of his body. 'You've come to a dead end. There is no more to—'

'It's a cul-de-sac, Nathan,' she insisted firmly. 'Someone, somewhere, knows more than has so far been told.'

'You have to face it, Brianna—more than will ever be

told,' he corrected harshly. 'And we can't live our lives on what might—or might not!—one day come to light.'

'We can't have a relationship that ignores that fact, either,' she stated stubbornly. '*I* can't,' she added.

This situation was complicated enough already, her feelings for Nathan undeniable; it would be wrong to complicate it further by becoming even more involved with him. If they should turn out to be related—in any way—having to let him go would be too painful to bear.

'But you can't deny this, either,' Nathan pushed forcefully, before his mouth came down hard on hers, demanding, passionate, completely possessive.

No, she couldn't deny this, she inwardly conceded, even as she responded to him instinctively, her lips opening to his, her arms moving about his waist as she clung to him. And she had once thought of Nathan as the Ice Man! He was heat, fire, burning passion—and Brianna was caught up in the flame!

Her throat arched as his lips travelled its length, those lips warm now against the top of her breast, above the neckline of the royal blue dress she wore, hands moving restlessly up and down her spine as he curved her body into his.

His eyes were dark as he looked down into her flushed face. 'I want you, Brianna. I want all of you. Naked and warm in my arms as I—'

'We can't, Nathan.' She somehow found the strength to weakly protest. 'I just can't do this!' Her eyes were full of unshed tears as she looked up at him.

His arms tightened. 'You want me too. I know you do!' he groaned.

She swallowed hard. 'I've never said that I don't—'

'Then forget about everything else and let me love you,' he demanded.

She wanted to, oh, God, how she wanted to! 'I can't!'

She wrenched painfully away from him. 'I just can't, Nathan.' The hot tears began to fall down her cheeks.

His expression was savage as he reluctantly released her. 'I'm not going to let you go, Brianna. Not because of this. If it means so much to you to know who your father was—'

'You *know* why it matters, Nathan!' she protested brokenly.

'Then I'll find out the answer for you!' he concluded as if she hadn't spoken.

Her eyes widened. 'And just how do you intend doing that, when no one else seems to have succeeded in doing so?'

'I don't know!' His voice rose agitatedly. 'I just know I have to do it!'

She shook her head, remembering Rebecca's letter, the things she had said about her baby's father. 'You could hurt a lot of people in the process,' she warned. 'Rebecca wouldn't keep me because of the people who would have been hurt if she did so, and without me she had no reason to go on.'

'And aren't we being hurt right now? I'm going to find out who your father was, Brianna—and then we're going to get on with our relationship!'

Brianna stared at him. He meant to do it; she could see that by the determination in his face. Nothing she or anyone else had to say was going to stop him…!

CHAPTER NINE

'How much did you say?' Brianna stared at Peter Landris as if he was an alien from outer space.

His mouth quirked. 'I believe you heard me the first time, Brianna.' He stood up, moving to a decanter and glasses that stood on the dresser, pouring a liberal amount of brandy into one of the glasses. 'Drink this,' he instructed her gently. 'And then we'll continue this conversation.'

She took the glass from him, her hand shaking slightly as she swallowed down some of the fiery liquid.

A million pounds!

It was beyond wildest imaginings. Beyond reason. Beyond everything!

'That is the amount of money that was left in trust for you by Rebecca,' Peter Landris continued calmly as he resumed his seat behind his desk. 'Of course there is the interest over the last twenty-one years to add to that amount, which makes a total of—'

'Please!' Brianna held up a silencing hand, a hand that still trembled. 'The initial amount is too much to contemplate just in itself, without adding any more.' She shook her head dazedly.

'Rebecca wanted you to have it,' the lawyer reminded her. 'It's a gift of love from her to you.'

'It didn't buy her happiness,' Brianna pointed out bitterly.

Peter Landris gave an acknowledging frown. 'Knowing Rebecca, she didn't expect it to do that for you, either. She just wanted to make sure you were able to take care of yourself, if the need ever arose.'

A million pounds would take care of that! It was inconceivable, an amount Brianna couldn't even think of as being real.

She had deliberately made this appointment for late on Monday afternoon, at a time when his father had assured her Nathan wouldn't be in his own office; now she wished he were here, after all. She needed something—somebody real—to cling to. But when she and Nathan had parted last week she had known she had to stay away from him, that it was better for everyone if she did. Except that she needed him so badly!

'Have you and Nathan argued?' his father questioned as he seemed to read her thoughts.

Brianna gave him a sharp, guarded look. 'Not exactly,' she replied reservedly. 'What makes you think that?'

'Your request that you see me when Nathan was in court, for one thing…'

'And for another?' She continued looking at him warily, sensing there was more.

'Nathan himself. My son isn't usually as—volatile as he's been the last few days.'

She had to admit, a volatile Nathan was a little hard to imagine. And yet, remembering his repressed anger when he'd driven her home last Wednesday night, perhaps it wasn't… 'In what way is he—volatile?' She made her own tone deliberately casual.

'"Explosive" probably better describes it. And I've been reliably told he's being ruthless in court at the moment, too. So what happened between the two of you to cause this?'

Nothing had happened between them, and that was probably the cause of Nathan's tension at the moment.

It hadn't happened because she hadn't dared let it. And she hadn't been too happy about that decision the last few days herself!

'I would have thought you would be pleased by the fact that we're no longer seeing each other,' she challenged Peter Landris, deliberately not answering his question; that was between Nathan and herself and didn't involve anyone else, least of all his parents!

Peter Landris sat back thoughtfully in his chair. 'And what makes you think that?'

She shrugged. 'I'm Rebecca's daughter—'

'And Joanne's granddaughter,' he reminded her warmly.

'Exactly!'

Peter shook his head. 'My brief—romance with Joanna may have been a mistake, Brianna, but I always cared about your grandmother. We may have married other people, but I always maintained an affection for her, and she for me,' he said gruffly.

'And how did your wife feel about that?' Brianna asked challengingly.

'I hope that you will come to know Margaret a little better over a period of time.' He spoke affectionately of his wife. 'You see, I told Margaret of my relationship with Joanne before we were married. Oh, yes, Brianna, I told her,' he repeated as she stared at him in open surprise. 'It would have been unfair of me to do otherwise. I couldn't have married Margaret, keeping a secret like that from her.'

'And what did she say?' Brianna breathed shallowly.

He smiled. 'Well, obviously she forgave me; as I told you last week, we've been married for more than forty years now!'

Knowledge of that brief relationship with Joanne couldn't have been easy for Margaret to accept. But she had accepted it, and their marriage was obviously a good one. Perhaps she had misjudged Peter's wife.

Brianna shrugged. 'I'm glad about that, but I still very much doubt your wife would feel too enamoured of her son being involved with Joanne's grandchild.'

'My wife realised long ago that Nathan is a fully grown man, and that if she wanted to keep her closeness to him she would have to keep certain of her opinions to herself!' Peter Landris's rueful tone implied it had been a hard lesson for Margaret to learn—but that she had learnt it! 'As for myself, I was a little concerned at first—but now I can't think of anything I would like better than to have Joanne's granddaughter in love with my son.'

'I'm not in love with Nathan!' Brianna defended heatedly, some of the colour returning to her cheeks.

'Aren't you?' his father challenged gently.

'No,' she returned forcefully. 'I— It's an impossible relationship.' She stood up agitatedly, needing the movement, needing to get out of there!

'Why?' Nathan's father persisted. 'I'm sure Joanne, and Rebecca too, would have been happy about it.'

'There's nothing to be happy about,' Brianna insisted. 'And we have no way of knowing how Rebecca would have felt about anything—she isn't here to tell us!' If she were, things might not be quite this complicated! 'Although I'm sure Giles wouldn't be at all happy about it,' she added pointedly.

'Giles...' Peter repeated thoughtfully. 'Nathan stayed with us over the weekend, and he called on Giles yesterday evening.' It was a statement of fact, but the look Peter Landris gave Brianna was openly questioning.

After their conversation last week, and Nathan's determination, she could guess only too easily why Nathan had been to see Giles. But she had no intention of discussing that with his father...

'Did he?' she answered evasively. 'I think, after what you've just told me, that I may have to go and see him too.'

Peter Landris frowned. 'Rebecca's legacy to you has nothing to do with Giles; it came originally from your maternal great-grandfather.'

'Nevertheless...' Brianna said. 'I feel I should discuss it with him.'

The lawyer didn't look at all happy with this suggestion. 'It's your decision, of course—'

'It is,' she echoed firmly, holding out her hand to him. 'Thank you for seeing me today. I—' She broke off as the door banged open behind her, not in the least surprised when she turned and saw Nathan standing there.

Even his father didn't look surprised to see him this time, a smile curving his mouth as he looked across the room at his son. 'You seem to be possessed of some sort of instinctive knowledge of when Brianna is going to be here,' he drawled mockingly.

'My case finished early,' Nathan answered him, but his gaze was fixed on Brianna.

'And?' his father prompted.

'My client won,' Nathan dismissed uninterestedly. 'You're looking well, Brianna,' he complimented her gruffly.

Considering her surprise at seeing him, and the shock she had received earlier concerning the trust fund that had been left to her, she found that slightly unbelievable. Although, she had to admit, it was wonderful to see him again. Perhaps he felt the same way about her...?

'I was just going,' she said tersely.

'I'll drive you wherever you want to go,' he replied automatically.

'That seems to be becoming a habit.' Her smile faded. 'I'm not sure it's one we should continue.'

'I wasn't asking you, Brianna,' he rasped harshly. 'I was telling you!'

'Nathan!' His father was the one to protest at his aggression. 'Must I remind you that—'

'You don't have to remind me of anything where Brianna is concerned.' His son glared across at him. 'Brianna is your client. She's here on official business.' His mouth twisted scornfully. 'My decision to drive her home is official too—I just made it so!'

Peter Landris had been right; 'explosive' did describe Nathan's current mood. The Ice Man had melted completely in the face of his heated emotions!

Poor Nathan, he was as unhappy as she undoubtedly was. What a mess this all was...

'Nathan, you've been storming about the countryside the last few days, visiting an assortment of people,' his father put in soothingly. 'Your mother is still reeling from your visit at the weekend and early departure this morning.' He shook his head. 'It wouldn't have been so bad if you had spent a little time with us, but as it was—'

'I had things to do—' Nathan announced impatiently, his gaze still fixed on Brianna.

It wasn't just fixed, it was devouring, the heat of his gaze actually seeming to be eating her alive!

'And people to see,' his father finished for him. 'We know that you went to see Giles last night. But your mother telephoned me a short time ago to complain you had been asking the household staff the strangest questions too. I don't know what's going on, Nathan, but—'

'I do,' Brianna admitted wearily, shaking her head and turning to Nathan. 'This isn't the way.' This way all he was going to do was antagonise and upset people. And that wasn't going to help anyone.

His mouth thinned. 'What other way do you suggest?' he demanded.

She sighed deeply. 'If I knew that, I would be doing it myself...'

'Exactly what is it you're trying to do, Nathan?' Peter Landris looked hard at his son. 'Besides wearing yourself down to an emotional frazzle!'

Nathan arched dark brows at Brianna. 'Shall I tell him, or would you rather do it?'

She would rather this conversation just ceased. But she could see by the older man's expression that he wasn't going to let it rest there. 'Nathan mistakenly believes that he—'

'Nathan *knows*,' he put in firmly.

'Believes,' she repeated stubbornly, 'that he will be able to succeed where Giles and I have both failed.'

Peter Landris showed his puzzlement. 'In doing what?'

'Finding out who Brianna's father is,' Nathan supplied.

His father looked startled. 'Why do you want to know that?' he said uncertainly.

'Because until Brianna knows the answer to that riddle she refuses to allow our relationship to follow its natural course,' Nathan burst out with barely contained anger.

'This "natural course" being?' his father probed.

'How the hell do I know?' Nathan returned crossly. 'Brianna has called a halt to our finding that out until she can be absolutely sure we aren't related to each other in some way!'

'Related?' Peter Landris looked more stunned than ever. 'But in what way do you think the two of you could possibly be related?'

'Cousins,' Nathan supplied abruptly. 'I think for a while she even imagined we might be brother and sister—until she met Mother, that is, and realised you would never have dared be unfaithful to her!'

'Don't be disrespectful about your mother, Nathan.' His father masked his confusion behind a show of anger, both he and Brianna avoiding meeting each other's gaze—because even though the two had only been engaged at the time, Peter *had* been unfaithful to Margaret with Joanne. 'I realise she can seem a little—stern at times, but she only wants the best for you.'

Nathan gave a weary sigh at the rebuke. 'I'm sorry. I'm afraid all of this is doing nothing for my temper.' He moved further into the room, dropping down into one of the chairs before running a tired hand over his eyes.

'Obviously,' his father acknowledged dryly, before turning to Brianna, his expression instantly softening. 'My dear, I had no idea you were thinking anything so—complicated. Of course you and Nathan aren't related by blood—'

'How can you be so sure of that?' she returned sharply.

'You see.' Again Nathan sighed heavily, shaking his head. 'Brianna believes she could be Uncle James's daughter. Because his middle name was Brian,' he explained, as his father looked totally confused now.

'I see.' Peter Landris's frowning brow cleared. 'Rather flimsy evidence to go on—'

'That's exactly what I said,' Nathan agreed.

'That's because you're both lawyers,' Brianna told them disgustedly. 'If someone were in front of you, standing over a dead body, a bloodied knife in their hands, you would still say it wasn't proof they were the murderer!' She glared impatiently at both of them.

'That's because it isn't,' the older man acknowledged. 'Every murder case is different. But the person who finds the dead body invariably moves that body, and, more often than not, picks up the murder weapon too. That doesn't make them the murderer. Any more than my brother James having Brian as his middle name must make him your father.'

'But—'

'It's impossible, anyway. And I'm surprised you didn't remember this yourself, Nathan,' Peter Landris added with reproof, unconcerned when Brianna and Nathan looked at him sharply. 'I'm sorry, Brianna, but the year you were conceived my brother James and his family were still living in America.'

'Hell!' Nathan swore angrily. 'I had completely forgotten!'

His father nodded. 'They returned home the following year because Samantha was due to start school.'

Elation. Utter and complete elation. She wasn't related to Nathan. She looked across at him with bright eyes, eyes full of a love she hadn't dared let blossom into fruition.

'I'm sure you may have something in thinking your chosen name has significance.' Peter Landris continued to talk in what had become an electrically charged silence. 'But it probably only has significance for the people involved...'

She blinked, turning her attention back to the older man with effort. 'What do you mean?'

'Well... Lovers, I believe, very often name pet names for each other.' Peter Landris looked uncomfortable now. 'When Margaret and I were first married, we called each other— Well, I believe it's quite customary to have affectionate terms of endearment for each other,' he amended hastily, obviously embarrassed as he recalled these names he and his wife had for each other.

'Brian is hardly a pet name—or, indeed, an affection-ate endearment,' Nathan scorned dryly.

'I'm just trying to be helpful!' Once again his father hid his awkwardness with the situation behind a show of anger. 'I hope I have been of some help to you, Brianna?' His expression relaxed as he looked at her.

She beamed at him, her relief at not being related to Nathan paramount. 'You most certainly have,' she confirmed with husky gratitude, inwardly wondering if the Ice Man could be termed an affectionate endearment...!

'You see, Nathan,' his father addressed him briskly. 'You were asking that particular question in the wrong places!'

'So it would seem.' Nathan grinned, standing up to hold out his hand to Brianna, the two of them smiling glowingly at each other as she stood at his side.

'Where are you going?' Peter Landris demanded quizzically, half standing as they walked towards the door.

'I believe,' Brianna answered him, 'that we are about to let our relationship follow its natural course.'

'Oh.' The older man dropped back into his chair. 'Well... I'll see you in the morning, Nathan,' he added lamely.

His son glanced back at him only briefly. 'Possibly,' he acknowledged enigmatically.

Brianna giggled once they were out in the corridor. 'Now you've shocked your father!'

'I doubt that,' Nathan muttered dryly, keeping a firm hold of her arm. 'He was young once!'

And when he had been young he had had an affair with Joanne, Brianna's grandmother... That sobered her slightly, her feeling of uncertainty returning. Okay, so she and Nathan weren't related, but there was still a lot of secrets between them that shouldn't be there...

'Hello, you two,' Roger Davis greeted them with a smile as he strolled towards them down the corridor. 'Your father still here, Nathan?'

'He certainly is,' Nathan confirmed.

His uncle came to a halt beside them, eyeing them both questioningly. 'You two look very happy.'

'We are,' Nathan replied firmly, his arm moving possessively about Brianna's shoulders.

Roger quirked grey brows. 'Do I hear wedding bells?' he teased.

'Not yet.' Once again Nathan was the one to answer him. 'But I'm working on it!'

Brianna turned to him with widely startled eyes. Marriage…? They had never even discussed the idea of marriage! She couldn't marry anyone when her life felt such a tangle…

Roger looked as surprised as Brianna felt, a dark frown now on his brow. 'I had no idea things had progressed this far…'

Neither had she! This wasn't letting their relationship take its natural course; this was jumping ten steps ahead of where they were now!

'I shouldn't worry on that score, Roger, neither did I!' She deliberately made light of it. 'I shouldn't believe everything Nathan tells you,' she added wryly. 'He isn't himself at the moment.'

'No?' Nathan raised dark brows. 'Then who the hell am I?'

'I'm not sure.' She moved out of his grasp.

'I seem to have put my foot in it.' Roger Davis winced awkwardly.

'Not at all,' Brianna assured him, anxious to put him at his ease once again. Besides, she couldn't even look at Nathan. 'It was nice to see you again, Roger, but I'm afraid I have to go now.'

'*We* have to go now,' Nathan corrected, retaining a firm hold on her arm even though she had moved out of his embrace.

Roger nodded. 'I'll just go in and see Peter for a few minutes.'

Brianna maintained a stubborn silence as she and Nathan walked down the corridor, but when she glanced back briefly down the corridor it was to see Roger Davis still watching them, a thoughtful expression on his face.

'Now look what you've done!' Brianna turned angrily on Nathan once they were outside in the private car park. 'Your uncle Roger will tell your aunt Clarissa, and then your aunt Clarissa will tell her sister—your mother!—and then—'

'So what if he does? And she does?' Nathan responded in a dangerously soft voice.

'Then your mother will confront you with the information!' Her eyes flashed.

'And?'

'And then you'll have to tell them all that it isn't true,' she snapped. 'Because it isn't true, Nathan. We may have established that your uncle James wasn't my father, but there are still a lot of complications to our forming a lasting relationship!' The fact that he didn't know of his father's affair with her grandmother and she did, for one thing! It was the sort of secret that people in a loving relationship shouldn't have between them... But it wasn't her secret to tell.

'The fact that you're now an heiress, for one?' Nathan remarked caustically, his eyes glacial.

Brianna became very still, looking at him steadily. 'I'm going to pretend I didn't hear you say that.' She spoke evenly, the flat tenor of her voice masking her inner pain. Nathan couldn't really think—

'I'm sorry, Brianna. Really sorry.' He shook his head as if to clear it, reaching out for her, his hands falling impotently at his sides as she moved away from him. 'I don't even know why I said that.'

'Because of the situation, Nathan,' she burst out. 'It's as I've said all along, this can't work between us—'

'But you know we aren't related now. What else—?'

'All of it, Nathan,' she bit out grimly. 'We both need to know all of it before we can... We would be building our relationship on quicksand.' She shook her head. 'I don't want that lift home, thank you, Nathan. I need to walk. To clear my head. To think.' Her elation of a short time ago had completely vanished in the face of her uncertainty.

'And then what?' He looked at her with narrowed eyes.

'That's why I need to think!' She groaned, her head starting to ache now. Was she just being silly? She didn't know any more!

Nathan didn't look reassured by her answer. 'This is my future you're deciding on too, you know,' he reminded her. 'I love you, Brianna. And I want to marry you.'

Nathan loved her...!

God knows, she loved him. Was it enough? Could they build their future together on that alone?

What happened if—or when!—her real father chose to reveal his identity to them? What happened then?

'I have to go, Nathan.' She turned away heavily, her movements disjointed. 'I have to go!' she choked before she began to run. Away from Nathan.

When all she really wanted to do was run into his arms and stay there. For ever...

She didn't know where she went, where she walked, whether she saw anyone she knew. She vaguely recalled drinking a cup of coffee somewhere. Knew that her legs ached from the amount of walking she had done. Knew too that it was dark by the time she arrived home.

There seemed to be more cars than usual parked outside the house—one of them she easily recognised as Nathan's Jaguar!

How long had he been there? What did he want? Because the hours she had spent walking aimlessly had changed nothing; she still had no idea who she was. Or where she was going!

She could hear the murmur of voices from the sitting-room as she quietly let herself in, leaning instinctively back against the front door as the sitting-room door opened and someone came out into the hallway. Gary... And he looked as if he was enjoying himself immensely.

'You aren't throwing a party, are you, Gary?' she teased as she stepped forward into the hallway.

'Brianna!' he greeted her warmly. 'No such luck!' He grinned in answer to her question. 'I've been dispatched to make tea. Your Nathan is great by the way; he's promised to take me for a drive in his Jag later.'

Her younger brother had a passion for stylish cars, and the promise of the drive was obviously compensating for having to make the tea. 'He isn't *my* Nathan, Gary,' she corrected.

Her brother shrugged unconcernedly. 'He said he was,' he returned casually.

'Then he said wrong,' she said firmly. 'Er—how many people are you making tea for?'

'Including you and me?' He did a quick count in his head. 'Six.'

Six...? Nathan and her father made four—so who were the other two people in the room? 'Gary—'

'Can't stop, sis,' he told her hurriedly. 'Poor Dad is up to his eyes in it in there; the conversation started to flounder about ten minutes ago and now they're basically just sitting there, staring at each other!'

But who were 'they'?

Her brother obviously wasn't about to tell her; he was disappearing in the direction of the kitchen. Once he'd returned with the tea and told them she was back there was going to be no escape for her, either. She might as well go into the sitting-room now and get this over with.

But who, exactly, were 'they'...?

Gary was right about the conversation having dried up; no one was talking as she walked into the room, but the tension could be easily felt. Her father sat in his usual armchair, but he sat forward, his hands gripped tightly together in front of him, not in the least relaxed, his expression grim. Nathan had dismissed the comfort of an armchair altogether, standing tensely by the fireplace, his expression even grimmer than her father's.

The other two people in the room sat side by side on the sofa, tightly holding each other's hands. Clarissa and Roger Davis. What on earth were they doing here?

But as she looked at the pain in Clarissa's blue eyes, saw the anguish in Roger Davis's face, she suddenly knew exactly what they were doing here...!

Roger Davis was the man Brianna had been searching for, the man who had the affair with Rebecca, the man who had fathered her baby.

Roger Davis was Brianna's biological father!

CHAPTER TEN

ROGER DAVIS!

It seemed incredible to her. He and Clarissa seemed to be so much a couple. She had liked Clarissa when she'd met her that weekend, didn't like the feeling now that she—her existence—was the cause of that pain in the older woman's eyes.

And Roger had told her he didn't have any children!

More specifically, he had said he and Clarissa didn't have any children...

Had he known then she was his daughter? Peter and Nathan seemed to have had no difficulty recognising who she was just by looking at her, had known she was Rebecca's daughter; surely the man who had fathered Rebecca's child must have been able to realise who Brianna was too?

He had known last weekend. He had to have known. So what was he doing here now? Could it possibly be because of what Nathan had said to him earlier this evening, about his intention of marrying her?

'Nathan?' She glanced at him uncertainly, not sure she wanted to hear what any of these people had to say.

'It's all right, my love.' He came immediately to her side, his arm protective about her shoulders.

It wasn't all right. It might never be all right again. She hated the man who had fathered her, felt after speaking to Giles that it was Rebecca's lover who had really let her mother down in the end. But Brianna knew she had liked Roger when she'd met him. And she couldn't

173

fuse the two into one person in her head. As for Clarissa...!

Brianna turned to her, admiring the way Clarissa sat so palely composed, so very much the lady still—in spite of the fact her world must be crumbling about her ears. 'Clarissa—Mrs Davis—'

'Clarissa will do, my dear,' she assured Brianna softly. 'I knew you reminded me of someone last weekend.' She gave a ruefully downcast look.

'Rebecca...' Brianna said weakly, wondering how this woman could possibly sit through this.

Clarissa smiled, a smile tinged with poignant sadness. 'No,' she refuted gently. 'It's Roger you remind me of. It's the stubbornness of your jawline, of course,' she continued. 'Roger can be very stubborn too, my dear. As he was twenty-two years ago, when I offered to release him from our marriage.'

Twenty-two years ago...? When Brianna was conceived. Had Clarissa known of Roger's affair with Rebecca even then? Oh, God...!

'It will be all right, Brianna.' Nathan's arm tightened reassuringly about her shoulders.

She looked up at him with bewildered eyes. How could he possibly say that? His uncle was her father, and although that meant they weren't related by blood, he was still Nathan's uncle...! Nathan's family were going to hate her!

'Darling, come and sit down.' Her father stood up to come to her, sitting her down in the chair he had just vacated. 'You've had a couple of hours to come to terms with this situation,' he reminded Nathan pointedly as the younger man looked concerned. 'It's still a shock to Brianna.' Her father turned back to her worriedly. 'Hear them out, Brianna,' he said. 'And try not to judge until you know all the facts. I don't think there are any really black villains in this, just a lot of unhappy people, and some of what you hear may sound vaguely familiar.'

She frowned her puzzlement at his last statement, but with Nathan standing guardian at the back of her chair, and her father kneeling to hold one of her hands, she felt cocooned by their loving care. Perhaps it was going to be all right after all...

'Tea.' Gary burst noisily into the room with the laden tray.

'His timing has always been impeccable,' his father said dryly to their visitors. 'Pour the tea, son. Hand it around. And then sit down and be quiet!'

Gary grinned good-naturedly and poured the tea uncomplainingly. If Brianna knew him—and she most certainly did!—he didn't in the least mind serving the tea, so long as he could be a party to what was going on.

'I think I should be the one to tell—Brianna—exactly what happened twenty-two years ago.' Roger Davis stood up, his movements restless, not looking at any of them, seemingly unable to do so.

'Be kind to yourself, darling,' Clarissa told him. 'You're only human; that doesn't mean you're bad.'

He gave his wife a shaky smile at her loving understanding, before turning quickly away again, his gaze fixed on the flowery wallpaper over the chimney. 'Twenty-two years ago, Clarissa and I had been married for five years. A very happy five years. The one jarring note for both of us was, even though we had never taken precautions not to have children, nothing seemed to happen in that direction.'

Brianna's father squeezed her hand. The familiarity. He and Jean had tried for years to have children of their own too...

She squeezed her father's hand back in acknowledgement, knowing how well he must be able to relate to what Roger was telling them.

'Months of tests later,' Roger Davis continued evenly, 'it was discovered that we would never have children of our own. I—it was a blow to us both. Although that doesn't excuse what I did next—'

'Roger,' Clarissa cut in sharply, 'I asked you to be kind to yourself,' she reminded him. 'You haven't told them everything about those tests. Or the hurt you received.'

He looked across at his wife with pained eyes. 'They don't need to know all that—'

'Yes, they do,' Clarissa insisted firmly. 'I realise you're trying to protect me, but you're doing it at a price to yourself. And too many people have already suffered for my teenage wildness.' She looked across at Brianna with tear-wet eyes. 'Roger is not a bad man. And I won't have you thinking that he is.'

He was a married man who had had an affair, an affair that had resulted in a child—her!—a child he hadn't wanted, along with her mother; how could Brianna possibly think good of him?

Clarissa drew in a shaky breath as she saw the scepticism in Brianna's expression. 'I believe I told you last weekend that I was the black sheep of my family? Well, during my teenage years,' she continued at Brianna's nod of confirmation, 'I was incredibly wild. I tried it all—drink, soft drugs, men. It was a disastrous relationship with one of the latter that finally sobered me down. I became pregnant,' she sighed. 'And, because I was involved with several men at the time, I had no way of knowing exactly who the father was—'

'Now you're being unkind to yourself, Clarissa,' her husband interrupted.

She gave a sad shake of her head. 'I'm being truthful.

I was nineteen, I didn't want my life cluttered up with an unwanted baby, and so—' She swallowed hard. 'I was away at university at the time, and it was quite easy for me to go—somewhere and have an abortion without my family ever having to know about it.' She gave a convulsive shiver at the memory.

'Quite easy!' she repeated with revulsion. 'It was the worst experience of my life. I'd had no idea! I was ill for weeks afterwards, didn't look after myself, and was finally admitted to hospital with a severe infection. What I didn't realise was that I would never have another child, that those complications had made me sterile. That was discovered five years after I married Roger and we had that series of tests. At that stage I owed it to Roger to tell him the whole truth. All of it.' She stopped to sigh. 'It was a terrible shock to him to learn how promiscuous I had been in my youth. I—for several months our marriage hung in the balance, as Roger battled inwardly to try and overcome his pain and disillusionment.'

'Enter Rebecca,' Brianna easily guessed.

'Enter Rebecca,' Roger echoed grimly. 'And I will not have any excuses made for my behaviour, Clarissa,' he added firmly. 'I was a married man and Rebecca was eighteen, very much in need of someone to love, and for someone to love her—'

'As you must have felt you were,' Brianna's father put in softly. 'I can relate to what you're saying, Roger,' he added with gentle compassion. 'There but for the grace of God...'

'Daddy?' Brianna looked at him frowningly.

'Relationships are very fragile things, my darling,' her father told her gruffly. 'And believe me, your mother—Jean—and I had our fair share of upsets in the years before we were able to adopt you. There's an awful lot of guilt—on both sides—attached to not being able to have a child of your own.'

'And then you had me.' Gary's cheekiness helped to ease the tension that had steadily been building in the room.

'And then we had you,' their father confirmed. 'And if that isn't a deterrent to having your own children, I don't know what is!' he teased affectionately.

'You have a wonderful family, Brianna,' Roger told her.

'I know it.' She squeezed her father's hand once again.

'Then also know,' her father spoke to her once again, 'that the deeper the love for your chosen partner in life, the deeper the rift when you aren't quite in kilter with each other. And that rift can sometimes seem like a chasm that you have no hope of crossing.'

Loving Nathan as she did, and after the altogether senseless argument they had had earlier this evening, she was beginning to realise that for herself...

'I'm not proud of my affair with Rebecca,' Roger continued frankly. 'It was just something that seemed to happen. A vulnerability on my side, a need on Rebecca's.' He shook his head at the memory. 'It seemed right at the time—but when Rebecca told me she was pregnant, I realised it was Clarissa that I loved, whom I wanted to spend the rest of my life with, even though we could never have a child of our own. I realised, given the chance to have that child of my own, that Clarissa's past no longer mattered, that I just wanted our future to be together. I—I had to tell Rebecca that.' He swallowed hard. 'And then I had to tell Clarissa about my relationship with Rebecca.' His eyes were deeply shadowed at the memory. 'I was hated by Rebecca. And forgiven by Clarissa.'

'I don't know if you can understand this, Brianna,' the older woman spoke to her gently. 'But Roger's relationship with your mother somehow made us equal again. This doesn't sound very fair to Rebecca, but somehow our marriage was stronger for all the pain, rather than weaker.'

'Too much pain has been caused already,' Rebecca had written to her. But Rebecca hadn't hated Roger. If she had, she would never have gone away, she would have stayed where he would have had to watch his child growing up, never able to acknowledge it as such. No, she hadn't hated him; she had gone away and had her child adopted, so that she wouldn't cause Roger and Clarissa any more pain...

'I do understand,' Brianna told Clarissa throatily.

'Can you also understand that I would gladly have become your mother?' Clarissa said emotionally. 'You were Roger's child, the child I could never give him. I would gladly have brought you up as my own.'

She had been wanted by so many people, it seemed. Rebecca. Giles. Clarissa and Roger. Graham and Jean. Not just an unwanted child, after all.

'I was stunned and then elated when Clarissa told me that twenty-two years ago.' Roger was the one to take up the story once again. 'But by this time Rebecca had gone.' He looked very sad. 'None of us managed to find her, despite months of searching. And then it was too late.' Roger swallowed hard. 'Rebecca was dead. And her baby had been legally adopted by a couple called Gibson. For a while I toyed with the idea of trying to get the baby back.' He gave Graham an apologetic glance. 'But that would have been pure selfishness on my part, and I had already let Rebecca down enough. She had chosen the people she wanted to bring up her child and I had no right to interfere in that. I had no rights whatsoever...'

Brianna couldn't argue with that, although she could understand his pain. 'Where did the name Brianna come from?' She frowned. Now that she knew Roger was her father, she could see no connection at all.

His mouth twisted grimly. 'It was our way of meeting,' he admitted, with a pained frown in his wife's direction.

'It's all right, darling.' Clarissa put a supportive hand on his arm as he stood beside her.

'It isn't all right,' he said self-disgustedly. 'But it's the way it was!' He looked across at Brianna. 'Rebecca didn't think our real names should ever be used in our conversations, and so when I rang her at home she would always call me Brian. Don't ask me where the name came from!' He shook his head. 'It was just a name she picked at random. If I said Brian wasn't available then she would know I wasn't able to meet her, and vice versa,' he dismissed impatiently. 'It all seems so childish now. But the name itself was of no significance, Brianna,' he added apologetically.

'But don't you see? It had significance for Rebecca,' she pointed out eagerly. 'If she had really hated you, she would never have given me a female version of that name. And she knew that one day we would meet—perhaps she even hoped you would see the significance of her choice of name—'

'How could she possibly know we would meet?' He shook his head. 'I think you're seeing things here, Brianna, that just aren't—'

'But of course she knew,' Brianna insisted. 'She left her will with your senior partner, with instructions for me to be contacted when I was twenty-one. She knew we would meet, Roger, and I also believe the reason she gave me the name Brianna was that she forgave you. Even if I never knew who you were, you would surely realise that I was the child she had been expecting when she left home—a child she had given the female version of a fictitious lover's name. She forgave you, Roger,' Brianna told him with certainty. 'It's the only reason she would have named me as she did.'

Clarissa spoke wonderingly. 'Darling I think Brianna is right.'

Roger sat down abruptly next to his wife. 'I'd like to think you were both right. I really would!' He shook his head, his face haggard with emotion.

Brianna looked at him, but she looked at him anew now, with the knowledge that he was her biological father. A grey-haired man in his early fifties, with kind blue eyes—eyes the colour of her own, she now knew—a man who had made a mistake in his life, a mistake that had changed the pattern of several lives including his own. It was a mistake he had had to live with for twenty-two years...

Wasn't it time it all stopped?

She swallowed hard. 'I forgive you.' She spoke huskily. 'As I firmly believe Rebecca did. You can't actually *be* my father—because I already have a rather wonderful one of those.'

'You most certainly do,' Roger agreed admiringly. 'And I'm damned sure I couldn't be as magnanimous as him, given the same circumstances.'

'As I said earlier,' Graham said softly. 'There but for the grace of God...'

She had never needed to be told what a wonderful father she had, but at that moment her heart overflowed with love for him. Thank you, Rebecca, she said inwardly.

'You can't be my father,' she repeated gruffly to

Roger Davis, 'but hopefully we can get to know each other. All of us, I mean.' Her gaze included Clarissa, her admiration for the other woman immense.

'And when Brianna agrees to marry me, you can officially be her aunt and uncle.' Nathan spoke up briskly.

Brianna looked up at him with glowing eyes. 'I think there may be some explaining to do with the rest of your family before that can happen!'

'Not really.' Nathan shrugged dismissively. 'Why do you think Roger came here? Because my father has always known,' he instantly supplied. 'And when he and Roger talked this evening he told Roger he had to do something about the situation—before I did someone physical damage!' he added self-derisively.

She looked at him with wide eyes. 'Does your mother know too?'

'Apparently.' He nodded, looking across at his aunt and uncle for confirmation.

'Margaret is my sister, Brianna,' Clarissa explained huskily. 'She and Peter were told the truth about Rebecca's baby long ago.'

Perhaps that explained Nathan's mother's coolness towards her that weekend! It had had nothing to do with Nathan and everything to do with worry for her sister's happiness. Perhaps, given time, once she realised that Brianna wished no harm to either Clarissa or Roger...?

She squeezed her father's hand one more time before standing up and going round the chair to stand at Nathan's side. 'In that case,' she said slowly, 'of course I'll marry you. I love you so much, Nathan. So very much,' she told him emotionally, knowing that she would always love him, that she had found lasting happiness where Rebecca hadn't. And that she had Rebecca to thank for giving her that happiness. She would never forget the woman who had given birth to her...

Nathan breathed in a ragged sigh of relief even as his arms moved possessively about her. 'I love you too, Brianna. So very much,' he echoed, as emotionally.

'Oh, boy.' Gary spoke up once again. 'What a wedding this is going to be!'

They all laughed at the understatement, relieved to have something to laugh about.

And Gary was right; what a wedding this was going to be...

EPILOGUE

SHE read the letter once more, a single sheet of note-paper, blotched with the occasional tearstain. It seemed so little, and yet it had given her so much. The rest of her life...

'Are you ready to leave, darling?' Nathan spoke gently behind her.

Brianna turned to him glowingly, her face alight with the love they shared. A love they had only hours ago confirmed in church as they were married. She was now Mrs Nathan Landris.

Everyone she loved had been there: her father and Gary, Giles, Roger and Clarissa, Margaret and Peter, Sam and Susan. With the third generation they had at last become a family united in love. And it was Rebecca's child who had united them. The money Rebecca had left for her daughter had been placed in trust for her grandchildren, when they arrived. Brianna could hardly wait until the day she would hold Nathan's child in her arms.

As Nathan stepped forward he saw Rebecca's letter in her hand, at once understanding the tinge of sadness he had seen in her eyes when he entered the room. 'She was with us in spirit, love,' he said gruffly as he gently took Brianna into his arms.

'Do you really think she knows how happy I am, how happy we all are at last?' She frowned her uncertainty.

'I really believe it,' Nathan assured her with certainty.

'I hope so,' Brianna said fervently.

'No more sadness now,' Nathan instructed as he

wiped the tears from her cheeks. 'Everyone is waiting for you to throw your bouquet!'

And it was with much laughter and teasing that Sam was the one to catch the sweet-smelling bouquet Brianna threw seconds later from the top of the wide staircase.

She had left for the church earlier today from the home she shared with her father and Gary, but Giles had insisted his granddaughter's wedding reception be held at the Mallory house. A much improved home. After years of letting it stagnate and crumble before his eyes, Giles had had the house completely redecorated, so that it was now light and airy—a suitable home for Brianna and her new husband to visit, to bring her children to one day too.

It seemed that Rebecca had given them all a new beginning.

And, as Brianna looked lovingly at her new husband, a man she wouldn't have met if it hadn't been for Rebecca, she knew Rebecca had given her the best new beginning of all...!

Take 2 bestselling love stories FREE

Plus get a FREE surprise gift!

Special Limited-Time Offer

Mail to Harlequin Reader Service®

P.O. Box 609
Fort Erie, Ontario
L2A 5X3

YES! Please send me 2 free Harlequin Presents® novels and my free surprise gift. Then send me 6 brand-new novels every month, which I will receive months before they appear in bookstores. Bill me at the low price of $3.49 each plus 25¢ delivery and GST *. That's the complete price, and a saving of over 10% off the cover prices—quite a bargain! I understand that accepting the books and gift places me under no obligation ever to buy any books. I can always return a shipment and cancel at any time. Even if I never buy another book from Harlequin, the 2 free books and the surprise gift are mine to keep forever.

306 HEN CH7A

Name	(PLEASE PRINT)
Address	Apt. No.
City	Province	Postal Code

This offer is limited to one order per household and not valid to present Harlequin Presents® subscribers. *Terms and prices are subject to change without notice. Canadian residents will be charged applicable provincial taxes and GST.

CPRES-98   ©1990 Harlequin Enterprises Limited

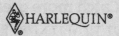

Not The Same Old Story!

Exciting, glamorous romance stories that take readers around the world.

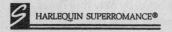
Sparkling, fresh and tender love stories that bring you pure romance.

Bold and adventurous— Temptation is strong women, bad boys, great sex!

S HARLEQUIN SUPERROMANCE®
Provocative and realistic stories that celebrate life and love.

HARLEQUIN® AMERICAN ROMANCE®
Contemporary fairy tales—where anything is possible and where dreams come true.

HARLEQUIN® INTRIGUE®
Heart-stopping, suspenseful adventures that combine the best of romance and mystery.

Humorous and romantic stories that capture the lighter side of love.